The Unpredictable Colors of Love

by

J. Arlene Culiner

Dedication

With thanks to Christine Arribas for the 1997 challenge, and to Bernard Tisserand and Yves Besnard who urged me to accept this new one.

Chapter One

"This is France?"

Fat raindrops slapped Callie's face, and a wild, gusting wind buffeted the cement platform. All she could see on her right was a sodden town; on the left, drenched fields and waterlogged vegetation.

"How about a glowing golden sun?" she muttered. "And where are those gorgeous olive trees? The vineyards stretching to an azure blue horizon?"

The wrong region...obviously. Was coming here another wrong decision? Perhaps. She'd been the only passenger to leave the train. Who in their right mind would come to a place this soggy? "I would," she grumbled. But she was used to making bad choices: she'd been doing that for almost an entire lifetime.

No option other than braving the elements, fighting her way through the murky yellow-brown puddles to reach the drab train station that seemed to be miles away. Head bent, suitcase rolling along behind her, long backpack with art supplies slung over one shoulder, she forged on ahead.

Soon her troubles would be over: someone would be there, waiting to drive her out to the Château de Froideval. Perhaps Nicholas Trier? Come on! A man as famous as Nicholas Trier had more important things to do than meet trains. Besides, it was better he didn't see her like this. Rain had trickled under her jacket collar, soaked her clothes, and converted her chic chignon into mousey rat's tails. Not the way you want to look when you're about to meet someone...astonishing. And so charismatic. Someone who'd made your heart go pitter-patter and whose intense gaze had suggested he wasn't immune to your own charms.

Finally. She was here. She jerked open the station door.

And stepped into an empty, frigid, rather dirty waiting room. No welcoming party, no smiling faces, and, of course, no Nicholas (*told you so*). In one corner, a heap of abandoned cardboard boxes sagged; on the left, a ticket window was permanently boarded up with shabby laminate panels. This place looked as though it had been closed for at least a century and a half. The only sign of life was an automatic ticket vending machine smugly humming its monotonous tune.

Now what? Perhaps someone was waiting for her out in the street. Dropping the backpack beside her suitcase, she went to the streaked station window and peered out. No waiting car, no bus, no taxi out there. Just rain gushing down with gusto and swirling in torrents along a street lined with tragic gray stone buildings. Not a soul around, either. Was this an abandoned, forgotten part of the world where the austere architecture testified to human life long since extinct? *Of course it isn't.*

She fought down discouragement. Still...facts had to be faced: no one, absolutely no one, had bothered to come and meet her train. She'd been forgotten, not only by Nicholas, but by everyone else, too. She glowered at the ticket machine—it was the liveliest thing around. "Now what am I supposed to do?"

The contraption just kept humming away.

Of course, she could call the château. If she found a telephone…because, as she'd noticed just before leaving the train, she'd forgotten to charge her cell phone, and it was now as dead as a dead cell phone can be. How unlucky could you get? Bad luck: once it sauntered into the picture, you couldn't just shake the dreary thing off.

She squashed the negative thought. Better find a public phone—did they still exist? No phone booth here in the station, of course. That would make life too easy. In her forty-eight years of experience, life had never been easy.

Again, she surveyed the street and saw nothing. Normal. How could you see anything through that torrent? She'd have to go outside, take a look. Leave her bags in here, unattended? Why not? What self-respecting thief would be out in this sort of weather? *A madman.* The thought didn't even faze her; a kook was better than nothing.

Then, quite suddenly, a man appeared, looming up from nowhere. Head lowered against the downpour, he pushed open the station door, entered, stamped his feet. From the depths of despair, Callie's heart zipped up into pure relief. So she hadn't been forgotten after all.

Of course, he wasn't Nicholas Trier—oh yes, she remembered everything about Nicholas from their one and only meeting in London: golden hair, chiseled features, a fine mouth. And how she'd reacted to the sight of him! An elemental gut reaction. Primitive. Female to the perfect male of the species.

This man standing in front of her was not of that same perfection. He was anything but a tall blond god.

Close to her height, his eyes and hair were brown-black, his hairline had receded, and he was solidly built with a broad chest and a thick, bear-like torso. No, no Prince Charming, yet at the moment, he was heaven sent.

"Thank goodness you've come for me," she blurted out in English. "I'd almost given up hope…" She stopped abruptly, realizing her error. She should be speaking to him in French. "Ah, pardon…mais…"

The man eyed her with what could only be astonishment. Then, slowly, a crinkly smile spread across his face. "Is that so? I never thought I'd hear those words from a charming stranger." There was only the tiniest inflection, hinting that English wasn't his first language, yet the grammar was faultless.

Callie swallowed, confused. Was it his tone, or the raw amusement in his dark eyes that told her she'd made a terrible mistake? Or was he poking fun at her because she'd sounded so ridiculously excessive? She hoped so. Time to make herself clear. Fortunately, she could do so in English. "I thought I'd been forgotten, but…" She stopped, assailed by doubt. "You have been sent to meet me?"

"I have?" His eyes were still glinting.

She felt like punching this arrogant, smug guy. "To take me to the Château de Froideval."

"Ah." The smile faded somewhat. "I'm afraid not."

"Oh." It was all she could come up with. She felt her flush of embarrassment. What an impression she must be making: red-faced, soggy, flat-haired, wearing dripping clothes, and babbling nonsense. Callie stood up as straight as possible. When you resembled a soaked vole, and you've just come out with provocative-sounding words that an unknown man has taken in the wrong way, only a show of cool dignity could help. "You didn't come to meet my train?"

"Most definitely not." His chin indicated the cardboard boxes slumped in the corner. "I came to pick up those packages of gardening tools."

"Ah." Her spirits sank even lower.

"Someone was supposed to meet you?"

"That's what I understood," she said miserably. *Or misunderstood?* She'd called the château from London, had given the man who'd answered the phone her arrival time. She'd done it correctly, hadn't she? Perhaps…perhaps not. Garbling something on the telephone in inadequate, home-schooled French, a language she hadn't practiced in years and years, didn't guarantee comprehension.

"You could give them a call," the man suggested in a kindly way. "You probably have a cell phone like pretty well everyone else in the world."

"I do." She sniffed. "The trouble is, it isn't working. Battery's dead."

He frowned with what might have been commiseration. Or simply indifference. "I see." He headed over to the bundles in the corner.

If she hoped to get out of this situation, she had to be bold. "Of course, if you let me use your phone, I'd be grateful," she said to his back.

Bending down, he heaved the boxes into his arms, then turned to her. "I'm sure you would be. Only one hitch: I don't own a cell phone." He didn't even bother hiding his contentment.

Callie gawked, open-mouthed. Who didn't have a cell phone these days? Who was this guy? What kind of place was this? Boarded up ticket windows, empty streets, miserable weather, and no phones. What had she let herself in for?

As if catching her thoughts, his smile broadened. "I'm a backward sort of chap." He didn't seem in the least distressed about it, either. "But this is a very backward part of the world." Despite the unwieldy heap of damp cardboard in his arms, he nevertheless managed a Gallic shrug.

He was pulling her leg, of course. He had to be, but Callie couldn't think of one single clever or snarky riposte, so she had to make do with another, "Ah."

"Of course, I could drive you out to Froideval. I'm going right by the main building."

She blinked. *Right.* Did he think she was idiotic? Climb into a car with a total stranger in a totally strange country? That was a first-class solution for a bad luck day. Who was he? He hadn't been sent by anyone at the château, so why should she trust him? Sure, he seemed nice enough—at first glance. But if he were a reincarnation of Jack the Ripper and scouting about for an easy victim, he was going to sound as sweet as caramel…at first, anyway. "I wouldn't want to put you to any trouble."

"No trouble at all."

"Don't worry about me. I'll find a solution. I can take a taxi. There are taxis here in town, aren't there?"

"There's a taxi service, yes. One taxi, one driver: Jean-Pierre Lacon. But you'll have to phone him because he lives eight kilometers away from the town center. Of course, you don't have a phone, so you can't call. And even if you did have a working phone, the trip out to Froideval by taxi would cost a small fortune."

"Oh." She could hear bad luck snickering: it had strolled back into the picture and was now leaning against the wall, smugly paring its nails. "There must be a bus, then. Or perhaps someone will be along to fetch me any minute now. I'm sure that's what will happen." The words tumbled out too quickly; she sounded desperate.

Those deep, dark eyes sparkled. "No buses. But you're right to hesitate. I could be anybody."

Just what she needed: Jack the Ripper with telepathic powers. "You could be," she agreed.

"I'll tell you what. How about if we stow your bags and these tools in my car, then cross the road and have a warm, inoffensive cup of coffee at a tiny, very original sort of café. Madame Besnard, the proprietor, can vouch for my spotless character. You can also call Froideval from there, have someone confirm my fingerprints are on file, and that I'm usually a pretty safe guy."

Callie felt both silly and relieved. She smiled, somewhat weakly. "I'm sorry for being so suspicious."

"No problem. You don't know me. You're a stranger here."

"And it's very kind of you to offer to drive me all the way out to the château."

"Not kind at all," he insisted. "I live only a stone's throw away, but you couldn't know that because you're not a local."

"Definitely not a local. No local would speak French as badly as I do."

He winked. "You'd be surprised." He shifted the cardboard box, freeing one hand, which he held out to her. "I'm Michel Alexandre."

She shook his hand, inwardly smirking: didn't everyone know the French were always shaking hands? Or heartily kissing you on both cheeks. "And I'm Callie Patterson."

"Pleased to meet you, Callie."

"Not as pleased as I am to meet you, Michel. What would I do without you?" And, again, she felt like kicking herself. Why was she always coming out with these embarrassingly excessive statements? She saw he was grinning at her.

"You know what I mean," she corrected. But her shoulders had relaxed, and she was less wary now. Somehow she had decided to trust this kindly stranger—despite her better judgment and her jangling early warning system. "Okay, Michel Alexandre, lead on, although dear Madame Besnard might be your henchwoman. If so, she'd be more than willing to give an axe murderer a good character reference."

"Very true," he agreed with evident cheer.

****

Five minutes later, they were in an oddly empty café that was more like a living room than anything else—and a very strange living room, at that. Some things had surely changed in the centuries since the French Revolution, but nothing in here was younger than a hundred years old.

A wood-burning stove ticked out heat from the middle of the room, and the odors of coffee, woodsmoke, and dried flowers floated on the air. Above the wooden wainscoting, walls were cracked with age and yellowed by old nicotine.

"What an incredible place," Callie said, and she meant it, too. "I never dreamt that I'd see an old, untouched café like this one."

Michel looked proud, as if it were his own creation. "I'm glad you like it. I certainly do. There aren't many such locales left. Most people seem to prefer all that's modern and impersonal."

An elderly, rather solid woman appeared in a doorway at the back of the room, and when she spotted Michel, she harrumphed. "Look what the cat's dragged in."

He feigned hurt. "That's a kindly welcome, if I ever heard one."

"Serves you right. I thought you'd forgotten all about me. It's always the same. People are fickle and unfaithful." But despite her words, the woman was obviously pleased as punch to see him.

"You're right to chew me out," he teased. "It's been almost three whole weeks since my last visit." He went up to that truculent lady, cupped her shoulders, and kissed her soundly on both cheeks.

"If you say so," she responded sullenly, although the corners of her mouth were twitching upward. "But here you are now. And in the company of a very handsome woman."

"Dear Madame Besnard, you make it sound as if I usually show up with the nightmarishly ugly." Turning to Callie, he pretended to see her for the first time. "However, I do agree on that point. A handsome woman indeed."

Puzzled, Callie scrutinized the two of them. She was fairly sure she'd understood the entire exchange, but who knew? It had sounded very odd. Perhaps a humorous reply would be the best way to cope. "I feel like a cow being judged at an agricultural show," she mumbled in very unsteady French.

"Normal," Michel replied, his expression tragicomic. "Men in this backwoods part of the world consider every living creature as livestock. Except other men, of course."

Madame Besnard turned to Callie. "Don't you believe a word of it. This region isn't worse than any other in France."

"Which is bad enough," Michel said with sham commiseration.

"Except that here it seems to rain more," Callie moaned.

"That's why everything here is so leafy and green," chirped Madame Besnard.

"Oh dear. What will my colleagues say when I come back to England looking like broccoli?"

"You'll be an even odder color if you don't dry out," said Michel. Taking Callie's elbow, he masterfully steered her toward a table and two chairs beside the hot stove. Then helping her out of her sopping jacket, he placed it near the heat.

Madame Besnard went into a back room, returned with two tiny cups of steaming espresso that she placed on the table. And folding her arms over her print housedress, she leaned back against the counter, inspected Callie pointedly. "Not from around here, obviously," she said.

Callie hesitated, scrabbling around for the correct phrasing. But who cared if a foreigner put verbs in the right tense or adjectives in their proper place? Her accent was as thick as swamp mud anyway. "I've just arrived from London, but I'm American."

"Do you live in England?"

"I do. My grandmother's second husband was English. My mother took me to England to visit them when I was five years old. Then, because she fell in and out of love with at least a dozen men every few months, she never did find the time to go back to the States."

"And when you grew up, you married an Englishman," Michel concluded.

"Is that a wild guess?" Callie asked.

"Yes, it is. But that's often the way people keep on living in other countries."

"I suppose you're right."

"And your husband hasn't come to France with you."

"I should hope not! We've been divorced for years."

"What a nosy man you are, Michel," Madame Besnard scolded before turning to Callie with yet another question. "And you're an artist, yes? You've come to France to spend a few weeks at the artist's retreat in the Château de Froideval?"

"True. But how do you know that?"

Michel gave another very Gallic shrug. "Madame Besnard knows about the retreat since, every June, a group of artists shows up. But the rest of the time, outside of organized tours to heritage sites and historic houses, strangers rarely darken the hills in this forgotten part of the country."

"Especially since the local cattle show is months away." Madame Besnard's cackle was unrestrained.

Callie had to laugh with her, yet she feared that being called an artist was rather deceptive. True, she did create delicate pastel drawings, and she'd shown them in group exhibitions at small galleries and cultural centers, but she had never been singled out for especial praise, notice, or success. *And pretty drawings, nice as they are, just don't cut the mustard in a dog-eat-dog art world.*

Michel was watching her with amusement mixed with a good dose of curiosity. "Your French is good for a foreigner, by the way."

Callie made a wry face. "Is it? I'm not sure I really understand what people are saying. And then I hear all my mistakes, and my accent is atrocious, and…"

Deftly, he cut into her self-criticism. "And you like to be perfect in everything?"

Did she? Perhaps. "Don't most of us want that? Yes, I know that perfection is impossible, but I do like to get as close to it as I can." And she was the sort of person who drove herself relentlessly. How could she do otherwise? It was part of her character, even though it usually made life harder than it had to be.

"Where did you learn French? In school?"

"No. From my grandmother. She lived in Paris when she was young. She was an art student, but she gave it up when my mother was born—women did that sort of thing back then. She said that having a baby was creative enough, but as soon as I was old enough to hold a pencil, she taught me drawing. And French, too. It was as if she wanted me to carry on from where she left off."

"You were lucky."

"I know that now, but I didn't back then. I liked learning to draw and paint, but French made no sense to me. None of the other kids around me had to learn it, and I wanted to be just like them. Therefore, I did my best to resist my grandmother's efforts." She sighed.

"To my immense regret today."

"Kids hate being different," he commiserated. "Have you spent much time in France?"

"Aside from a few visits to the museums in Paris, I don't know the rest of the country at all," she admitted. "Therefore, I can be forgiven for thinking this area would be a hot, dry, Mediterranean one. A few days ago, as I stood shivering in the English summer, I imagined that I'd soon be fighting off hordes of cicadas."

"In this area, we fight off fish."

Callie giggled. "Too bad I wasn't clever enough to bring along a snorkel and wet suit so I can work in the open air."

"Artists have to suffer."

There was a snort from Madame Besnard who was still taking in their conversation from her post at the counter. "Artists seem to think the public has to suffer, too."

Puzzled, Callie stared at the woman. "In what way?"

"Just ask him what he does." Madame Besnard jabbed an aggressive chin in Michel's direction.

Beaming with what appeared to be pure delight, he turned to Callie. "She's referring to my own paintings."

"You're also an artist?"

"Or so he claims!" Madame Besnard's hoot was gleefully malicious. "Don't let him fool you. An artist, my eye! You should see what he puts on those awful canvases of his, don't know what the world's coming to. Whatever happened to the good old days when people painted things you could recognize—portraits, children, animals, flowers, houses, and scenery? Not poor, horrible, blue things with two red eyes on one side of their head."

Leaning back in his chair, Michel roared with raw, undisguised hilarity. When he finally caught his breath, he said with mock seriousness: "Madame Besnard, our fine arts critic, has passed judgment. All I can say in my defense is that even poor, horrible, blue creatures with two red eyes on one side of their head, also like to have their portraits painted from time to time."

Chapter Two

The weather was less violent now that the wind had died, but the rain was a penetrating downpour, and the sky remained wretchedly grim. Michel was a calm and reassuring driver and, in his battered, noisy, and ancient teal-blue van, they followed a narrow road twisting lazily between dense hedges punctuated by rows of overgrown oaks, and interspersed with acacias, walnut, and chestnut trees. From time to time, they passed solitary granite farmhouses that crouched warily on the dark hillsides.

"Not a very welcoming sort of landscape," Callie declared. What an understatement! Gray houses, a gray sky, moss-green vegetation, deep shadows, sodden fields, wet air—and in the waning evening light, all was unrelentingly gloomy.

"Welcoming? I suppose I've never thought of this countryside in that way."

She realized how negative she must sound. She didn't want to offend Michel: this was, after all, his home territory, and he was so pleasant. And so incredibly helpful. What, in heaven's name, would she have done without him? "What I mean is, I can see how some people might find it...picturesque...in a way. But you have to admit there's an isolated, brooding feeling to it."

Which he would never detect, of course, because

he lived here. This is what he saw every morning when he woke up, when he opened the window, when he walked out of his front door, when he drove to work. She, on the other hand, wasn't fond of the rural world. No, it was worse than that. She heartily disliked endless green fields, stodgy lines of green trees, and incurably tangled green hedges.

"It's cheerier when the sun's out," said Michel. "That does happen sometimes, you know."

"I should hope so."

"Of course, sun's pretty rare in this part of the world." He looked sorrowful. "When it does dare show its face, it's to remind us that the rain is about to start again."

Callie almost whimpered with misery, but a quick sidewise glance told her he was fighting a grin.

"You are right about the isolation, though," he admitted. "This isn't a heavily populated part of France. It was always a very poor one—and that means that much of the beauty hasn't been destroyed by development. That being said, deforestation was disastrous back in the days when countless trees were hacked down to make wooden war ships."

"Those days are over, thank goodness."

"They are. But that wasn't the only way the environment was harmed. For hundreds of years, the land here, like elsewhere, has been victim to bad management. Wild areas were eradicated, chemicals were overused in agriculture, and predators like foxes, wolves, and snakes were exterminated. All that has resulted in a devastating ecological imbalance."

What could she say to that? She had no experience in the domain, for she was, most certainly, no country girl. Countryside was all this leafy lettuce-like stuff they were passing through now, or all the nasty woody areas that lay outside of London. She avoided the rural world assiduously—especially after marrying Malcolm, a man who also hated flowers, forests, and animals of any sort. Their life together had taken place in the heart of the dirty but comforting city, nowhere else.

Even after her divorce, she'd made sure that her surroundings were urban only. City streets, shops, welcoming pubs, teashops, libraries, museums, and art galleries, all of those reassured her. And now, here she was, ripped out of familiarity and wedged—albeit temporarily—into the vegetable realm.

"In order to reverse the damage," Michel continued, "I work with a dedicated team, replanting and rewilding. We turn dismal forestry plantations into broadleaf forests, protect what's left of old growth, and make conditions right for natural pastureland where birds, reptiles, and mammals thrive."

"That's the sort of work you do?"

"That's what I help do much of the time. We also remove dams, restore spawning areas, and encourage useful creatures that were almost wiped out—beavers, for example—to return."

"What for?" Callie asked. "I mean, beavers are cute and halfway fuzzy, but they saw down trees with their sharp little teeth, don't they?"

"Sure, they do. But when they fell trees along the river, they create ponds that attract insects, fish, as well as birds." He smiled, a man satisfied with his role in life. "I can't tell you how good it is to see fallow fields become woodland rich with lichens, orchids, wild garlic, hyacinths, and lily of the valley. On the lands belonging to the château, I replant hedges that have vanished, plant new trees in the places where older ones were heedlessly removed."

"It sounds…" She searched for the right word. Fatiguing? Endless? Difficult? Wholly unappealing? No, although they sounded apt to her, none of those would do. "It sounds like back-breaking work."

Beaming happily, he briefly turned to her. "Perhaps so. But it leaves me with enough time to watch things grow, listen to the wind, smell the sweetness in the air, relish the silence, the solitude, and particularly the isolation."

Okay, okay. His words did paint a pretty picture, one full of pungent herbs, hopping bunnies, and busy, humming bees. But she wasn't going to be charmed. As a child, she'd been forced to go down the mucky rural road with her impossibly fey mother, a woman attracted to scents, magic stones, bizarre lovers, spirit trees, gris-gris, gurus, and obscure New Age sects. The necessity of feeding and clothing her little daughter came at the very bottom of her list of important things to do. "Solitude never bothers you?"

"It's precisely what I crave as a lone wolf."

"Lone wolf?" she scoffed. "That can't be true."

He quirked an amused eyebrow. "How so?"

"You're too friendly. If you were a true loner, why would you make the effort to rescue me?"

"What male can resist a damsel in distress?"

He had a great smile, slightly lopsided, lightly self-mocking, and she did appreciate his easy manner, as well as the gentle teasing. How she loved men with humor! They lightened the atmosphere, made everything in life seem so simple.

Yet, none of the men she'd been with had ever had a sense of humor, and certainly not Malcolm, her ex. Somehow it was always the gorgeous, humorless men who attracted her. Men with the bodies of Greek gods. Egotistical, self-obsessed men who loved being the center of attention, who needed admiration from everyone. Why was she so drawn to them? Perhaps because, as an artist, she needed physical beauty around her.

"And because you're a lone wolf, you live in a lonely den in the middle of a deep forest," Callie jibed.

"Close." His eyes twinkled. "In a stone house well hidden under a hill."

"A wolf den," she confirmed. "Nothing like the Château de Froideval?"

"No, thank goodness."

"What's wrong with it?" she asked, alarmed.

"Nothing. But a big grand dwelling like that is very demanding."

"Especially since people can no longer afford to hire masses of servants," Callie added.

"Also, it's taken an enormous amount of elbow grease and investment to bring it back to its original state. I'm sure you'll enjoy staying there because it's a jewel these days. All the eighteenth-century charm is intact, and you couldn't wish for a lovelier setting, but only thirty years ago, it was almost a complete ruin.

"Really?" said Callie. "That's so hard to imagine. I saw pictures of Froideval on the Internet. It's beautiful."

She'd also searched online for photos of Nicholas Trier, and each time she'd found one, her heart had pitapatted a little faster. She'd devoured every article about the man, about his exhibitions, about those he arranged for others. Soon she'd be face-to-face with him again. Would he remember her? Would he look at her in the way he had during their meeting in London?

How silly those thoughts were! She knew nothing about Nicholas—other than the fact that he was unmarried and was considered an important artist. Successful bachelor artists always acquired fans, groupies, hangers-on, and ardent lovers with ease. Was that the case with Nicholas? She couldn't question Michel about him, could she? Or perhaps she could. Her curiosity always did win out.

"Do you know Nicholas Trier and his artwork?" Silly question. Wouldn't everyone—everyone who had an interest in the art world—know about Nicholas?

"Very well," said Michel briefly.

Callie waited, but he offered no other information. "I met him in London," she added as a prompt. A prompt that was a complete failure, for he still said nothing. She tried again. "He was having a show in the Ripple Gallery."

"And he told you about the retreat at Froideval?"

"No. I'm an assistant curator at the Glassover Museum. Nicholas showed up one day to discuss his art and the possibility of an exhibition, and one of the curators I work with told me about the retreat. The idea of getting away from London and concentrating on my drawing was irresistible, so I applied."

She didn't mention that her fascination for Nicholas had been a large part of that motivation: *I'm just a besotted fan, a groupie, an uncritical admirer of sexy Nicholas Trier. Why deny it*?

"And what do you think about Nicholas' artistic

work?" Michel asked.

Oops. She'd been hoping that no one would ask her that question. Now someone had, and she was truly on unsteady ground. What could she say? She could always hedge, couldn't she? Gnawing her lower lip, Callie sought inspiration.

"Well," she began, "some of it is rather interesting, I think." She hoped Michel wouldn't ask her *what* she found interesting because she wasn't sure she knew, and that was a major problem.

Why? Because she'd decided she *had* to like the sort of art Nicholas did. After all, she'd be working alongside him for the next two weeks, hearing his theories, learning about his creative ideas, perhaps soliciting his help. If she played her cards right…if she were very, very lucky…perhaps he'd help her along with her own artistic career. Wasn't that the most important thing?

She waited for Michel to question her further, but he was silent, and that was a relief. She didn't want to reveal her fascination for highly successful, ambitious men…men very unlike Michel.

Because she *had* noted what Madame Besnard had said back at the café—Michel was a less-than-successful painter. Not like Nicholas whose work elicited glowing reviews in the best art magazines, who'd had a show in one of the most prestigious London galleries.

Sure, Michel seemed like a rugged, dependable sort of guy, but you had to draw the line somewhere. He dug holes and planted trees for a living; he worked as a gardener. He was a country bumpkin.

Just look at this wrecked rust bucket of a van he

was driving. It bumped and jerked along the road with all the comfort of an antediluvian cement mixer. The raggedy upholstery was made of some kind of cheap plastic, and every single motor part whined and whistled in an agony of loose fan belts and fatigued plugs. Why, this age-old thing even had unlined corrugated sides! And those garden tools in the back were banging away on the metal floor with all the hysteria of an incompetent drummer gone mad.

Not that she'd condemn anyone for being poor. She'd grown up poor, and during her long marriage to Malcolm, she'd denied herself any luxuries, paying, instead, for his paints, brushes, and canvases, for his art studio, and for all his various art projects that had never quite panned out. Since then, she'd developed a healthy allergy to starving, unsuccessful artists.

They slowed as they drove through Épineux-le-Rainsouin, an inauspicious village of two-story slate-roofed houses with their picturesque stone walls ruined by a covering of yellow cement. Once outside, Michel turned right and they began clanking down a gravel drive, passing a shuttered gatehouse, then continuing on through an extensive park of dark, brooding trees. Finally, the van rolled to a cacophonous halt.

"Here you are. End of the line."

Callie strained to see through the murky evening light, then gasped. "It's…superb."

Stately and imposing, yet the late Renaissance manor was without pretension. Two identical wings with symmetrical rows of long windows led off a central building, and slits of welcoming yellow light spilled out onto the wet ground outside. What a blessing to find something so civilized in the midst of a rural backwater.

"Believe me, the photos I found on the Internet don't do justice to this place."

"We do our best." Michel climbed out of the van, hauled Callie's bags out of the back, and carried them up the broad, stone steps. She followed behind, thanking him profusely, but he waved her words away. "Just a question of being in the right place at the right time."

"And it was a pleasure meeting you," she said, and she meant it too. She looked over at him. My goodness: weren't his eyes captivating—a soft brown, like velvet.

"The pleasure was mine." He turned and headed back down the steps. "Good luck."

Good luck? Why do I need luck? Too late to ask now. With a strange feeling of regret, Callie watched the van clanking, banging, and shuddering its way back down the tree-lined alley before disappearing. She had enjoyed Michel's company, but would she ever see him again? Maybe. Hadn't he said he was replanting on lands belonging to Froideval? That meant he was employed here as its gardener, or as an estate manager of some kind. Did employed staff mix with the artists at the retreat? Maybe not.

Turning, she contemplated the immense carved door in front of her and pulled back her shoulders. Perhaps now her brilliant future would begin.

Chapter Three

Before her hand had even touched the heavy brass knocker, the door groaned open with a martyred, suffering sound, very much like that of a vampire's castle in some backward and utterly bizarre corner of the world. Except the flustered woman facing her was a decidedly modern creature.

Lugubrious thoughts of sinister mountains, coffins, and Dracula were forgotten—despite the woman's first despairing moan. "*Mon dieu.*"

It was hardly a welcome, and assuredly not an encouraging beginning. Nonetheless, it was up to Callie to sound normal—if she wanted things to run smoothly, or simply comprehend what was going on. "Hello. Uh…I'm Callie Patterson. I arrived by train and…"

"How distressing," the woman said in heavily accented English.

Callie gulped with astonishment. "Sorry?"

Bending, the woman grabbed the handle of Callie's rolling suitcase. "No, not you. I mean you're not distressing. Of course you aren't."

"I hope not," Callie muttered.

The woman frowned. "*Pardon?*"

"Just mumbling away." Good heavens! Who was this peculiar person? Although she didn't look at all odd. Probably around her own age—in her late forties or early fifties—she was slender and naturally classy in dark slacks and a white silky blouse. Her brown eyes were gentle, and her soft mouth hinted at good humor and smiles. One of those smiles appeared now.

"Come in, please come in. You have to forgive me. I am Azeline Dubon, and I think it's appalling that no one was at the station to meet you. Louis had to drive all the way to Erblon *pour dépanner* one of the artists whose car *est en panne*—euh...is broke down, and Nicholas' train is delayed in Paris and we have no key for his car, and—euh—who knows when he arrives. We were hoping you would call when you arrived, *et nous*, we'd have sent Jean-Pierre, our local taxi driver, to *cherche* you." The babble of mixed French and English stopped.

Azeline Dubon pursed her lips and paused before beginning again. "I'm sorry for my bad English. I will try to slow down. Things should come out better that way." She smiled rather sheepishly.

Callie smiled back. "Your English isn't bad at all. My French is much worse."

"That's normal. You are foreign."

"Incredibly true," Callie admitted.

"But why didn't you call? I was sitting here, waiting to hear from you." It sounded like a reproach.

"I forgot to charge my cell phone, so the battery was dead," Callie said. Then she looked around her. They were standing in a soaring entry hall, as grand as any ballroom, lit by a complex and beautiful chandelier. Straight ahead, a road-wide marble stairway led up to the higher floors. "But it doesn't matter. Everything turned out all right. A very helpful man—"

"Yes, of course. Michel brought you. I saw his van from the window. I hope you are not angry with us."

"Of course not."

"What a terrible way to start your stay here."

"Oh no," Callie protested. "Michel isn't terrible. He was very nice." Any gloom at being abandoned at the train station was forgotten.

Azeline Dubon's smile turned sly. "Yes, I don't mean Michel is terrible. Not terrible in a bad way. Women always like Michel. Very, very much. All women. He is…" She stopped, searched for the right words. "He is…what do you call it in English? A lady-killer?"

Michel Alexandre? A lady-killer? She had to be joking! Callie shook her head with vehemence. "That isn't at all what I meant."

But Azeline Dubon only threw her a knowing smirk. What was going on? Why was this woman dreaming up a romance? If so, she was on the wrong track. Not only that, but it was pretty hard to imagine a dark bear-like balding man as a successful seducer. A pleasant, friendly guy, yes; a lady's man, no.

Perhaps the answer to the mystery lay elsewhere: perhaps Azeline Dubon was secretly in love with Michel. Why not? There was an apposite German saying for this sort of situation: *Every pot has its lid.*

"Come, I'll show you your room." And before Callie could say another word, Azeline had grabbed her suitcase once more, and she was heading toward that sweeping staircase.

Clutching her artist's backpack, Callie raced after the woman who was—what? The housemother? The manager? Some other, as yet undefined, member of the staff? "Please, Madame Dubon, you don't have to carry my bag."

"Just making up for the bad start." Streaks ahead of Cassie, she had already reached the first-floor landing and was climbing to the second where, three doors down, she threw open a door. "And please, no Madame Dubon. Just call me Azeline. We're not formal here."

"Fine…Azeline." Callie felt uncomfortable using the first name. Why? Because they were in a château, and that urged formality and eighteenth-century manners?

"Here you are. No en suite in an old place like this, I'm afraid. The bathroom is at the end of the hall."

"No problem for me," Callie assured her. She had never been anywhere near luxury in her life. She remembered the creaking outhouses of her childhood—when outhouses were available. More often, improvisation had been necessary since her mother had chosen to live in fields, in a car, in squats, and longest, in a freezing un-insulated attic with no running water.

"Adding modern conveniences and adjoining bathrooms can be very costly," Azeline explained. "Especially since the upkeep of a place as big as Froideval is onerous. Not to mention how careful we have to be not to ruin the aesthetics with plumbing and additional walls. There are very strict heritage protection rules in this country."

Callie stepped into the room that would be hers for two weeks and almost gasped. She had never imagined anything quite like this. It was—exquisite—no other word would be adequate. At one end, a huge gold-framed mirror topped a graceful marble fireplace; two Voltaire armchairs covered in burgundy velvet stood on either side of the hearth. The high ceiling was embellished by cornices and coving; wooden floors were highly polished; and every piece of furniture—the huge wardrobe, a fine little writing desk, and a coiffeuse dressing table—looked as though they had been kicking around back in Marie-Antoinette's day. The bed, ornate and luxurious, was covered by a heavy white linen throw, and topped by large square softly inviting pillows. "Incredible," she breathed.

"Glad you like it," said Azeline, and Callie could see she was chuffed.

"It's so impressive, it will seem like a waste if I close my eyes and fall asleep here." How different from her cramped flat, from a whole life filled with ugly places. *And even this is only temporary.* Transient beauty that she had earned via her modest talent and habitual determination.

Azeline's voice cut into this last, less than pleasant, thought. "For me, it's very gratifying when people appreciate what we're offering. Believe it or not, some who come here are so blasé, they don't even take notice of their surroundings."

"I can hardly believe that. Especially if they're supposed to be artists."

Azeline shrugged, another one of those Gallic gestures accentuated by waving hands. "Why don't you get settled in, then come downstairs when you're ready. We'll all be in the winter garden having drinks before dinner, and you can meet the other artists who are here. Nicholas might be back by then."

As Azeline closed the door behind her, Callie went over to the high curtained window. Outside, in the dusky light, she could just make out the dense park, and those menacingly huge, spinach-green trees. And beyond, hazy, mist-shrouded hills rolled into the mournful distance. It was a landscape of mysterious dells, knotted hedges, and bottomless streams...and it wasn't at all comforting. Not to her, it wasn't.

Wistfully, she thought of her London apartment, the constant rumble of cars, trucks, buses, and commuter trains, the filthy air, the overhead airline chaos, and the noxious commotion of her idiotic neighbor's much-hated musical taste. Strange how, after only one day of travel, she was missing that familiar, ear-splitting world!

She almost kicked herself for her silliness. *Here I am, surrounded by pastoral beauty, and I'm homesick for city rumpus and dirt.* She pushed hankering to the back of her mind. *Get used to it.* She had to. *What choice do I have?*

She went to her suitcase, clicked it open. Time to change into dry, unwrinkled clothes. She pulled out a cotton skirt and pretty pink blouse. At least she'd look neat and tidy, as usual—although neither simple garment could disguise what she called her L-shaped body—tallish, no opulent curves to speak of, and very long, thin feet.

Then, sitting at the spindly legged coiffeuse, she tortured her still-damp hair into its usual neat chignon and corrected her light makeup. Well, this was the best she could do. *If my decidedly average looks don't capture Nicholas Trier's heart, I'll just have to rely on exceptional charm, brilliant wit, and dazzling intelligence.*

****

She'd first caught sight of Nicholas Trier—at a distance only—on an unusually frozen winter morning when London streets were as dangerous as sheets of reflecting glass. She had been in the museum's pottery section, working with two assistants, Mary and Suzie, rearranging a display of futurist, avant-garde Italian ceramics from the late 1920s. He had stood in an adjoining corridor in the company of Tessa Sharp, the museum's director, and although he hadn't turned in their direction, neither Callie, Suzie, nor Mary could have missed him.

Tall, golden, and elegant, every single gesture, albeit studied, was supple. And as he moved away with Tessa, he did so with a smooth, sleek strut.

"Do you see that?" Mary leered with carnivorous ardor.

"Mighty easy on the eye," added Suzie, with equally concupiscent fervor.

"And he knows it." Callie's snort was dismissive. "You can just tell."

"Yes, I'm sure he does, but that's to be expected," Suzie said with a know-it-all smile. "With looks like those, you don't see a monster each time you examine yourself in the mirror."

"And that's probably often," Callie riposted.

Mary observed her with undisguised curiosity. "Sounds like you're speaking from personal experience."

"I am. I was married to a pretty boy like that, and he hogged all the mirrors. No way I could get close enough to one to put on mascara. He signed his death sentence the day he told me he was more desirable as a man than I was as a woman."

Suzie sniffed. "Beauty slipping into the role of the Beast?"

"You've hit the nail right on its shiny little head."

Carefully, Callie settled a gaudily colored Riccardo Gatti vase in the display case. "So who is that particularly divine specimen we just saw with Tessa? And how has he managed to attract the attention of our esteemed, but usually unattainable, director?"

"His name is Nicholas Trier, and he's the French star artist of the moment," answered Mary with evident satisfaction.

"He is?" Callie blinked. The name Nicholas Trier meant nothing to her, and it obviously should have. Knowing who was who in the art world was part of her job. It was also her duty to herself, for her life had always turned around art. "What sort of work does he do?"

"He's another one of those who've been influenced by the conceptualists." Mary wrinkled her nose. Like Callie, she was partial to the more traditional forms of artistic expression—the work of Hockney, Freud, Crozier, Bacon, or Le Brocquy.

"Oh. That sort of thing." Art that didn't depend on actual painting, or the creation of sculpture; art that was always accompanied by convoluted explanatory texts called "documentation." Art that could—and did—look like anything: a table covered with dirty dishes, or blurred images collated by artificial intelligence.

Mary nodded. "And the reason Nicholas Trier's in London this week is because he has a show at the Ripple Gallery. The opening is tonight, so he's contacted Tessa. Most likely, he wants us to acquire and show his work here at the Glassover."

"I heard he's in charge of some sort of artist's retreat in France," Suzie added. "In a Renaissance castle, somewhere. Doesn't *that* sound like a treat?"

"It does," Callie confirmed.

"He also organizes exhibitions for other artists, those who aren't established but are part of his entourage." Suzie always knew about such things since she wrote articles about the art world for an online journal. "The group is called New Source. Thanks to Nicholas Trier, his artists show their work all over Europe."

Callie sniffed. *Some people have all the luck.*

****

What happened next was pure chance. That same evening, she'd been working late as usual, ensconced in the cramped and messy office she shared with four others, when Tessa had appeared in the doorway.

"Where is everyone?"

Callie observed her boss, baffled by the irritated tone. "It's six thirty. They've all gone home."

"Damn!" Tessa almost stamped her high-heeled boot. "In that case, you'll have to do it."

"Do what?"

"Go to Ripple Gallery for the opening of Nicholas Trier's show. Someone from the museum should be there, and this evening, I have to catch an eight o'clock flight to Berlin."

Tessa took in Callie's tidy coiffure, unremarkable navy blue sweater, and tweed skirt. "At least you look decent, although not radically fashionable—we both have to admit that, don't we?" Her smile was saccharine. "But you won't have to go home to change. Get to the gallery as soon as you can. The opening starts in half an hour. And make sure everyone knows you're there to represent the Glassover."

Packing herself into the crowded bus that struggled

through clotted traffic, Callie fretted. She was only an assistant curator in the pottery department of the Glassover Museum—a very tiny minnow who sloshed about in a pond filled to the brim with savvy sharks—so how could she replace the dynamic Tessa Sharp? What, in heaven's name, was expected of her?

But after she entered the gallery and fought her way through the opening night crowd, she stopped worrying about her boss, her job, and her role.

It was this man standing in the center of the room who drew all her attention…again. How could she help but stare? He was one of the most magnificent men she'd ever seen. A blue-eyed god, he glowed, and hidden under that tastefully cut tweed jacket, silk shirt, and corduroy pants, was the suggestion of a flawless male body.

Naturally, a crowd of admirers surrounded him. Female admirers. And collectors. And journalists. How could anyone break through a barrier like that? How could she capture his interest? What was she supposed to say? *Hi. I'm an assistant curator at the Glassover Museum, a very lowly figure on a big, tall totem pole.*

And just then, as she'd stood gaping, she'd felt a hand tug at her shoulder. It was Nina Portifo, the hard-nosed gallery owner. "Where's Tessa? Isn't she here with you?"

"No," Callie answered, somewhat embarrassed by her superior's defection. "She had to fly to Berlin this evening."

Nina's annoyance was palpable. "How annoying."

"Which is why I'm replacing her," Callie answered with a neat and synthetic smile. Although secretly huffed by Nina's tactless dismissal, she was rarely daunted by slights.

"Then we'll have to make do with you," said Nina ungraciously, and she pulled Callie forward, right into the circle surrounding Nicholas.

"Nicholas, this is Callie…uh…"

"Patterson," Callie supplied. She wasn't important enough for Nina, silly snobbish cow, to have remembered her name.

"She's a curator at the Glassover Museum," Nina continued smoothly.

And Nicolas had turned and looked at her. Really looked at her, his eyes, clear, piercing, locking with hers, until the surrounding air seemed to crackle with energy, and every single teensy nerve in her body tingled.

"Yes," Callie managed to say. "I saw you at the museum this morning." Why add that she had only been peeking at him from another room? Wouldn't it be better if he thought she was someone of importance?

"Callie," he said. His accent, sweetly French, turned her childish nickname into musical notes.

Her throat was dry; her senses reeled. He'd stolen her breath away, but she had to say something. She couldn't stand here ogling him like a besotted fool snagged by love at first sight. "Congratulations on this show," she'd croaked. And felt like kicking herself. Nicholas Trier didn't need *her* approval.

He ignored her words, and his eyes scanned her honey-brown hair in its neat chignon, lingered on her mouth, and his gaze was as tactile as an actual caress. "It is lovely to meet you." His voice, too husky, too sensual, spoke of more southerly climes, of racy evenings, and pungent, heady wines.

But before her addled brain could come up with a witty comment, a retort, a clever—or even stupid—question the crowd surged around them, and a woman, self-assured and evidently affluent, began talking to Nicholas about the show of his work that she had seen in Cannes. Callie was out of the running.

But in that microsecond before he'd turned away, his limpid gaze had met hers once more. And she had read promise there, and intense interest, and even regret that their meeting hadn't been more private.

"So you couldn't keep away either," said a voice in her ear.

Turning, Callie came face-to-face with her very smug colleague. "Mary? What are you doing here?"

"I could ask you the same question, but I think your answer would be the same as mine." Mary ogled Nicholas Trier.

"You're wrong," Callie riposted. "Tessa sent me here because she couldn't make it. She's flying out to Berlin this evening."

"Come on. Tessa told you that? You think she was planning on coming to this opening?"

"Why wouldn't she?"

Mary sniggered. "As we both know, Tessa bestows her favors as restrictively as any queen. However, since she wouldn't want to openly snub Nicholas Trier, an artist who is presently the toast of the art world, she sent you."

"You mean she'd never invite him to give an exhibition at the Glassover?"

"Correct. It's not at all the sort of art she'd choose. Go take a look, and you'll understand what I mean."

Callie began circulating through the gallery and did

her very best to appreciate what she was seeing—large printed words, half-words, single letters, invented words, and obscure phrases pasted onto the gallery's walls. Dutifully, she read the explicative documentation, and there was a great amount of it, but…well…she did find those texts wearisome. *Why does contemporary art rely so much on explanation?* Art was visual—at least to her it was.

Even after guzzling two glasses of unpleasantly acidic white wine (*and why doesn't a gallery as prestigious as the Ripple run to something better?*) she had to admit that she wasn't fond of Nicholas' work. No, she never had appreciated this side of the contemporary art scene. *So what? Does it matter? No one (except perhaps Tessa) will ask for my opinion.*

Besides, all the others in this overheated, overcrowded gallery were admiring. Nicholas Trier was the sort of man who would always be surrounded by cooing, clinging, rapacious fans—some had followed him here from France—and Callie would have needed a shiny, razor-edged machete to get anywhere close to him.

Yet she and Mary had stayed on, waiting at the edge of the humming crowd, until the bitter end. And doing that had paid off. Because they were swept along with fifteen others as they trooped over to a nearby Italian restaurant. Not that he was any more accessible, even then. He was seated so far away, at the very end of the long table.

"Have you noticed how often he looks at you," Mary whispered in her ear. She even sounded envious.

"At me?" Callie pretended confusion, but Mary was right. Nicholas Trier often glanced in her direction with definite interest. Why? Because he thought, as a curator at the Glassover Museum, she was an important contact? What other reason could there be? She knew she was even-featured and pleasantly attractive, but not remarkable. "How old do you think he is?" she asked, mostly to cover her confusion.

"Around fifty, perhaps. You interested?"

"Come on, Mary," Callie said. "Sure, we both think he's hot. But we also know that, aside from this one evening, there's little chance we'll ever see Nicholas Trier again. Thanks to our jobs at the museum, we're always meeting artists—local artists, artists who are passing through town, or artists who come from foreign countries. And we meet experts, critics, scientists, writers, and journalists. But even when the encounters are highly stimulating, they're usually one-off experiences."

"How true." Mary's tone was wistful, and Callie knew she was remembering that pale, ethereal painter-poet who, after a feverish three-day romance, had skittered back to Manchester, his wife, and three children.

Talk at the table had turned to people known in the art world, the investors, and to Nicholas' work. Openly, he basked in the attention. Of course he did! It was only when they were finally getting ready to leave, paying the bill, pulling on their winter coats, gloves, and scarves, that she found him standing beside her. No mistaking now: the interested glitter in his eyes was for her alone. What could she say that would make him remember her? What would single her out as a person of interest? She thought of what Suzie had told her that very afternoon.

"I heard that you run an artist's retreat in France."

"Because you are also an artist, Callie?"

That accent! That soft, almost mellifluous, tone. He had even remembered her name! Incredible. She melted completely. "Yes. I do my best. I manage to show my work from time to time." She tittered, a deprecating little sound. "Tell me about the retreat."

"The retreat is a place for artists to meet, to work, to discuss new ideas, and compare techniques. And sometimes..." He stopped, smiled. "Sometimes it is a place where artistic people come together to think, to refresh themselves."

And get close to you, thought Callie, but didn't say.

"If you are interested, you can get the information on my Internet site." His eyes searched hers, almost as if he hoped she would take this further...unless she'd been imagining things.

"I will," she'd promised.

Then he had been swept away—in a very proprietorial manner—by two tall, imperious women. And that was that.

****

That evening, after meeting Nicholas Trier, she'd opened her computer and found the information about the artist's retreat. It was a yearly event lasting two weeks and was indeed held in a eighteenth-century château. However, admission was limited to artists whose work had been approved by a selection committee. Too bad...

When a student, Callie had dreamed of becoming a professional artist and creating works conjuring up beauty, or joy, or controversy. But after marriage to the far more talented Malcolm, she'd taken a full-time job to support them both. Yet, her ambition still intact, she'd continued to draw, color, experiment...and hope for recognition.

Although convinced her pastel drawings would never pass muster with a selection committee, Callie had sent off her application and twenty photos of her work...then waited. *Just imagine!* Two weeks in which to further develop her skill! *Two whole weeks in the company of Nicholas!* What if she became part of his group, New Source?

Two months later, she received a letter telling her she had been accepted to the artist's retreat at the Château de Froideval. Incredible! The stars were finally shining on her. Her luck was up. And, now, here she was. In France. Finally. And about to be with Nicholas again.

Chapter Four

Although she had no idea how to find the winter garden, Callie couldn't miss the sound of bright chatter and tinkling glasses that reached as far as the entry hall. After passing through a majestic reception room with its several seating arrangements and large gold-framed landscape paintings, she found herself in a hot, damp glass house.

Since she often sketched in Kew Gardens' exotic Palm House as well as in city parks, she recognized some of the plants: red-hot cat's tail, lipstick plant, golden trumpet, and kangaroo paw. At least in here, as in Kew, nature was potted, domesticated, therefore unthreatening. No hirsute, smelly Tarzan the Ape Man would come swinging through the crowd on a carnivorous vine; no giant killer ants hid in the shadows, honing their lethal mandibles.

Instead, some twenty or thirty undeniably normal-looking people were gathered in this private rainforest. But, as if drawn by a hefty magnet, her eyes slammed toward the tall man standing near a wrought iron table and talking to a cluster of younger women. Her heart pounded; her lips ached. The magic was still here for her, so were excitement and longing.

How his broad shoulders filled out the tweed jacket, and ropy thighs shaped the designer jeans. That half-wild shock of hair begged for fingers to lose themselves in it; and the long, flat upper lip, the full lower, both suggested passionate kisses. No wonder all the women gathered around him were so besotted.

A luscious blonde was wound around his right arm like climbing clematis: full mouth, slanting cat's eyes, and a knowing look, as if Nicholas belonged to her exclusively. Perhaps he did…but only in a way. Because another, equally proprietary woman with midnight-black hair was entwined like honeysuckle around Nicholas' left arm.

Were those two members of New Source, Nicholas' exclusive artist group? Was glamor a prerequisite? If so, she was no competition for such determined femme fatales. Then she pulled herself up short. She couldn't just stand here gazing. Slowly, like a famished predator, Callie began crossing the room in his direction.

And he looked up. And their eyes locked. He was watching her in just the same way he had in London. She stopped when she was a few feet away from him.

"Hello."

"Hello to you, Callie. And *bienvenue*—welcome to France."

The timbre of his voice was as sonorous as she remembered. And he knew who she was; he had recognized her; he hadn't forgotten her. *Incredible.* "Thank you." Awed by the intensity of the blue gaze, she was breathless. And, once more, lost for smart or witty words.

"And no one was there to meet her at the train station, although we all knew she was arriving." Azeline Dubon was now standing beside them, and there was definite chastisement in her tone. Apparently, she wasn't one of Nicholas' awed fans. "You should have left us the keys to your car since you knew you wouldn't be around."

"Ah. How terrible of me. I'm so sorry…" Nicholas smiled into Callie's eyes and even managed to look contrite at the same time.

"Luckily, Michel happened to pass by the station, and he brought her back here."

The smile vanished, and Nicholas scowled at Azeline. "Michel did?"

"I was very lucky," Callie chirped.

Nicholas ignored her. "How very convenient." He sounded surprisingly terse.

Although he'd spoken in French, Callie couldn't miss the surly note. Evidently, Nicholas Trier and Michel Alexandre weren't on the best of terms. *Interesting*. She could appreciate why a gardener and a struggling amateur painter would be jealous of Nicholas, but why would Nicholas dislike Michel?

There was no time—and no way—to solve that mystery. A distinguished silver-haired server was now standing by her side, and he was holding a tray of tiny glasses filled with a coppery liquid.

"Bonsoir," he said with a cheery smile. "I'm Louis, the man who couldn't meet your train this afternoon. When you taste this potion, it will make up for any negligence. It's called *pommeau*, and it's a local specialty made from apples."

Before she could reach for one, Nicholas lifted a glass and handed it to her. And as she took it, their fingers met, briefly, definitely. How was it possible for such a light touch to be so searingly electric? She looked up at him. His eyes, meeting hers, had heated.

Inwardly, she shivered. With what? Anticipation? Lust? With the desire to submit to his powerful male aura? "Thank you," she managed to murmur. To hide her confusion, she lifted the glass and sipped the thick, sweet liquid. It was delightfully pungent, but before she could turn to the dignified Louis and say so, he had moved off, and Nicholas had turned back to the little group gathered around him. What was he talking about? Art, of course.

"The idea is the important aspect of the work. Strategies must be planned, for they're the very essence of creation. Actual execution is merely secondary."

"Thanks to conceptual art, I know that creation is limitless," added an unkempt fake blonde. "I don't have to paint or sculpt. I just need to be mentally agile."

At least, that's what Callie *thought* was being said. Was she misconstruing the conversation? She couldn't be sure. If so, it was the fault of her inadequate vocabulary.

Desperately, she tried to apply those half-forgotten childhood French lessons to an intricate debate about artworks consisting of messages in neon, furniture wrapped in yellow fur, and a video in which someone walked back and forth in an empty room.

Would all discussions at the retreat be like this one? She couldn't help wondering what she was doing here. *I'm just a hopeless traditionalist, out of step with what is really going on.* Why had her application been accepted? It was yet another mystery to solve.

"You are bored."

Was it that obvious? Embarrassed, Callie turned to the person who had spoken in English—a weedy man with pale beige hair, beige eyes, and beige skin.

"It's all a bit difficult to follow..." she began.

His sneer revealed two rows of crooked teeth. "It is boring, very boring. These people...all they care about are long discussions. Talk, talk, talk. If art becomes words only, that means a new Dark Age has started." And with that rather enigmatic, but strangely satisfying, declaration, he moved off.

Who was he? Another one of the artists, perhaps, although, to Callie, his clothes suggested he might be a handyman who had just come off the job: sloppy, floppy, beige trousers, a sagging gray-beige sweatshirt, and grungy sport shoes.

The problem was, many of the artists in the room (aside from the clinging vines) were similarly attired— *as if they've just finished cleaning out the garage.* Others wore yoga pants and loose tops in what was, apparently, the accepted current French style. In her neat, rather prim clothes, Callie suspected the others thought her an old-fashioned schoolmarm.

Most surprising, everyone came in all shapes and sizes: *and that puts to rest the silly notion that the French—particularly the women—are never bulky or overweight.*

This being ascertained, Callie drifted to the open door of the lush greenhouse. Outside, the pitch-dark garden was sodden under the persistent rain. Wouldn't it ever let up? Rain, muck, and gloomy skies might be ideal for gardeners, for tree and hedge planters like Michel Alexandre, but not for a pastel artist.

"You have settled in?"

The voice, deep and sexy, startled her. She turned, found Nicholas standing behind her. Why—she hadn't even felt the man approach. *You'd think, with his deep magnetism, I'd have sensed him.* "Settled in?" She searched her mind, scrabbling about for an interesting-sounding answer. Didn't find one. "Oh…yes…in a way. I've only just arrived, of course."

"Of course." His eyes blazed with pure charm. For her alone?

"And it would be nice if it stopped raining so I could go outside and work."

Although she hadn't said anything amusing, Nicholas chuckled, a deeply satisfying sound. "Then we will have to have a heart-to-heart talk with Zeus and see what he can do."

"Zeus?"

"The god of rain, thunder, and lightning."

"Oh, of course." Callie felt like kicking herself for her ignorance.

"Or perhaps our bad weather will make you change your approach to art."

"My approach?"

"You are certainly here because you are less than satisfied with your artwork, is that not true?"

She frowned, nonplussed. "I've felt less than satisfied with what I'm doing for some time now. But how could you know that?"

His smile was confident. "Because you are not unique in that feeling. Many who come to the retreat are searching for new approaches, a new way of working. The very best abandon what they've been doing, change their style, and philosophy."

"I see," she said cautiously. Did she?

"But don't worry," he said soothingly. "We all motivate each other. There are also many things to see in this area, and they, perhaps, will give you the inspiration you need. There are galleries and museums not far away. We can make excursions, also visit other artists' studios. It will be a good time for you."

"I'm sure it will be," said Callie, although she wasn't optimistic. How would she fit in?

Nicholas contemplated his little knot of admiring beauties. Then turning back to Callie, he lowered his voice one notch. "When all the excitement calms down, you and I…we will find moments for a tête-à-tête."

And with that promise in the air, he left her, returned to the others, to the bright chitchat, the discussions, and the arm candy. But her heart was thumping.

Nicholas had come to *her*, not to the others. He had proposed outings to *her*, had alluded to exclusive, intimate meetings in the future. *She* had been singled out for his attention, no one else. Yes, things were looking up, after all. Why worry?

****

"Meals take place in what was once the servants' kitchen near the back of the house, not here," said Azeline as she and Callie stood in the open doorway of the main dining room with its deep oriental carpets, long, finely worked table, and myriad chandeliers. "That's because this is one section of the house we show to tourists. As you can imagine, it always has to be immaculate."

"Tourists?"

Azeline wrinkled her nose. "A necessary evil. Froideval, like many heritage sites, has to open to the public during the milder months of the year. It's one way owners can keep these stately homes going these days. Tourism brings additional income, and it also ensures that grants keep flowing in. However, we only accept small, well-organized groups with very efficient guides, so it isn't much of a problem. Louis and I make sure that the screaming hordes with no interest in art, history, or culture keep away."

"I can see why people would want to come here, though. Everything is quite breathtaking."

"It is," Azeline agreed as she closed the double doors behind them. "Just make sure you keep your bedroom door locked for safety when the tour groups are around—in case someone gets too curious and decides to wander around on their own."

"Or gets lost." Callie waved her arm, a gesture that took in the endlessly long hallway in front of them where the paneled walls were lined with the portraits of forbidding-looking ancestors. "This place is huge. A place this size must cost a fortune in upkeep."

"True, but having Nicholas run the artist's retreat is just one way of getting subsidies. We also have local artists who come in to give courses all year round in the old carriage house. Not only that, all the outbuildings have been let out to ecologically responsible small enterprises."

"What can you tell me about Froideval's past?" Callie asked.

"No famous royal people ever tarried here, if that's what you hope to hear. But this building's history does nicely illustrate what happened in France over the last few hundred years."

"Go on."

"For a start, Froideval was constructed in 1748 for the Marquis François-Hyppolite de Bénou, but before that, a much older feudal castle stood in its place.

There's nothing left of it now, only a wall or two, and the faint trace of a remarkable, fourteenth-century wall painting. But back in the 1700s, the servants who worked here claimed that the ghosts of the former owners haunted the corridors at night, wringing their hands, wailing, and mourning the destruction of the earlier fortress-castle."

"Are they still around, those specters?" As much as Callie fancied the idea of ghostly figures lurking in historic buildings, she wasn't convinced she'd relish running into a few of them on a trip to the bathroom in the dead of night.

"Unfortunately, no," Azeline said, with a sorrowful shake of her head. "It would make life so much more interesting. They'd certainly liven this place up in the off-season. I'd love some spooky fun during the long, dull winter nights."

Callie snickered. "I'll bet tourists always want to hear about the ghosts."

"Of course they do," Azeline agreed. "People just love letting their imagination run away with them."

"And they adore being frightened. That's why they pile into fun fairs, or go to haunted houses, or flock to scary movies. Why else indulge in bungee jumping, or tightrope walking, or parachuting from planes?"

"Exactly. So you can imagine how excited visitors are when they learn that, after the Marquis François-Hyppolite de Bénou, and his wife, the Marquise Thérèse-Bonne de Livry, were guillotined during the Terror, there were even more ghostly sightings along the outside walls."

"How exciting, although I hope they stay outside."

"If those phantoms exist at all. Their daughter,

Flore, survived the Revolution, and she had the property restituted to her in 1799. She and her descendants managed to hang on here for well over a century. But because it was costly to run an estate without serfs, the only awful specters anyone ever saw in those days were the rabid debt collectors."

"Why did the family stay on?"

"I suppose they had nowhere else to go, but life couldn't have been easy for them. By the early twentieth century, Froideval had become an almost uninhabitable ruin, like many of the country's châteaux, strongholds, and manors. Many were bought up for very little money by the newly rich—people who thought that, by owning all the trappings, they would be sprinkled with the stardust of nobility. Some new owners even bought titles to solidify their newly acquired status."

Azeline opened her arms in an encompassing gesture. "So there you have it: French great house history in a nutshell. And now it's time I show you where meals are served or you, too, will turn into a ghostly figure." And she led the way down the hall to the back of the building and up a short stairway to a mezzanine.

****

If Callie was disappointed that she wouldn't be enjoying the dining room's high painted ceiling and fine tapestries, the servants' kitchen was so quaint that any regret changed to elation.

The stone floor, the uneven whitewashed walls, the exceedingly long wood-burning stove, all dated from Froideval's early days: this was the best example of a domestic museum. Terracotta pots stood on high wooden shelves, and hanging around the massive fireplace were menacing iron cooking instruments she couldn't even begin to identify. *And I wouldn't want to either. They represent hours of ungrateful toil.*

On a buffet table against the far wall, she found salads, breads, cheeses, fresh vegetables, nuts, and fruits. All looked fresh and savory, and Callie was relieved. She knew from hearsay that the French were dedicated meat eaters, and that they were now heedlessly exchanging their renowned gastronomy for greasy fast food, thereby greatly extending their waistlines. But here she could choose what she liked and keep to her vegetarian diet. *I won't starve, but I might overeat.*

She loaded her plate and carried it to a free place at one of the refectory tables where those already seated were guzzling bottles of red wine, ripping up chunks of bread and using them to wipe plates and knives clean, then cutting into melting cheeses or pâtés.

And, although loaded forks were also being heaved mouthward, chatter was as animated as it had been in the winter garden. It was just as hard to follow, too. Was she the only foreigner? Aside from two French-speaking Italian girls, it appeared so. The other artists seemed to know each other. Perhaps this was not the first time they had been to this retreat, or else they mingled in the country's various artistic circles.

"I am in Froideval three year," said Yvette, the small woman with straw-like blue and orange hair seated beside her. Her pointy, serrated knife slashing the air, she picked out others at the long table. "Here I meet with Bernadette, Lucienne, and Roger. We live in different part of France."

Yvette spoke with a heavy accent, and her English grammar was as doubtful as Callie's French grammar, but what a relief to put off her struggle during the meal. "And you all come here to work together?"

Yvette stopped cutting her slab of bright pink ham and eyed her suspiciously. "This is retreat. We are come to think, to change ideas. Some work, some don't work. We talk about projects."

"Ah," said Callie, feeling lost at sea.

"And you? You are here for working?"

"Yes," Callie confirmed. "I'm definitely here for working...um...I mean I'm here to work." If she didn't watch her step, her French might improve, but she'd end up speaking a far inferior sort of English.

"What work you want to do?"

"I'm a pastelist."

"You are working in pastel?" Yvette was so amazed, she forgot about the drooping morsel of meat dangling from the prongs of her fork. "What you are doing with pastels?"

"I do cityscapes. Buildings, old walls, and crowds." Callie suspected that this conventional answer would garner her no applause—not in a world where theory was prime.

Yvette's incredulity turned into something resembling derision. "How *ringard*...so old-fashioned."

"Yes," Callie admitted. "Very old-fashioned." And what of it? She loved the buttery feel of pastel under her fingers as she blended and smeared; she adored the wealth of grays, the depth of reds and browns that emphasized brick walls and recessed doorways, that made unrelenting matter come to life.

"The problem is, that too few people understand

pastel as an art tool," said a rounded cherub-like man with enviable angel's curls who was sitting opposite.

Callie sent him a grateful smile. Why engage in a battle about materials on her first evening here?

"People think pastel is only for children, or for amateurs," he continued, "condemning it as the inferior medium of the artistically inept. But look what Millet and Delacroix did with it."

"And Renoir. And Dégas, too," she added, then gawped, fascinated, as the cherub slathered a thick slab of butter onto a chunk of bread and topped it with an even thicker coating of fatty meat pâté.

Catching her stare, he became deadly serious. "This kind of pâté is called *rillettes*, and it is very popular in France. Do you know what *rillettes* are?"

"No." She didn't want to either. To her, the stuff looked and smelled very much like dog chow.

"It is made by boiling bacon, pork shoulder, and ham in much pork or goose fat for around two or three hours." Opening a cavernously large mouth, he pushed the entire food mass inside, and his chubby jowls puffed out like a squirrel's.

The concoction sounded rather blubbery and health threatening to Callie, but she didn't think that the man, so obviously engaged in masticating and swallowing, would be interested in getting her take on the subject. Instead, she loaded her own fork with carrot, chickpea, and palm heart salad and relished the tangy sesame vinaigrette dressing.

"I don't mean what I say to you in bad way," chirped Yvette, more charitable now, perhaps embarrassed by her tactless condemnation and the cherub's response. "It is just a little unusual. Anyhow, you must do interesting work if you are here. And Nicholas has approve you."

"He has?" Callie put down her fork. "I thought it was a committee that decided."

"This is very true. But Nicholas also must accept artists. How he can talk and work with if he don't like?"

"I see." Yet she felt strangely flattered. And very hopeful. "So Nicholas works with us while we're here?" For she had no idea how the retreat was run.

"Of course, no. We work alone. Some people work on project together. Many use computer to plan what they will do when they leave. One sculptor, Stephan, he work in the atelier. There are painters, too. But many of us are here to make connections, to exchange."

It sounded dull enough to Callie's ears. More talk, more theories, more struggling to understand. But hadn't Nicholas promised excursions? He had.

She glanced over to where he was sitting at another long table. He was, of course, surrounded by the usual gaggle of females vying for his attention. The seductive blonde was there too, perma-glued to one arm. The beddable brunette was joined to the other.

Suddenly, Callie felt dreary, jaded, and very much out of place. Perhaps it was just the fatigue of the long journey that brought on discouragement. Time to repair to that beautifully appointed bedroom upstairs and take comfort in the world of dreams. After all, tomorrow was (usually) another day.

Chapter Five

In the morning, Callie sprang out of bed, went to the window, and looked outside. Groaned. Green, that was the overriding color. Green grass, green fields, green trees, green hedges. *Yuck*. Green was fine for spinach, sprouts, cabbage, and broccoli, but as far as landscape went? *Yuck again*.

Not only that, it was still raining, and when she opened the window, she noted that the air was decidedly nippy for June. It was as though she had never left England. *Next time, I'll head for an artist's retreat in Mexico, or Senegal, somewhere nice and dry that guarantees sun.*

At least she had packed stout walking boots, jeans, and two thick sweaters, just in case—not that clumpy walking boots and straight jeans suited her, emphasizing her gawky Ichabod Crane shape. Well, she didn't have to dress like a farmer this morning, did she? Pulling on yet another neat skirt and pretty sweater, she made her way downstairs and headed for the old servants' kitchen.

Except...like any nosy, rude, and impudent tourist, she couldn't help opening a set of huge double doors and surveying the room beyond (although, from the rows of gold-framed paintings along the corridor, those sour, long-dead ancestors glared disapprovingly). What luxury a privileged group of people had known, and what beauty. Tremendous skill had created those carved wooden cabinets with their marquetry, and the tables and chairs with fluted legs. There were two porcelain pendulum clocks with ormolu mounts, and ornamental acanthuses decorated overhanging balconies, ceilings, walls, as well as vases.

How did people live in such a palace? Callie knew she couldn't. Every waking minute of every day would be fraught with fear—of stumbling recklessly across the waxed oak floor and shattering precious crystal, or sneezing and ruining fine gilding, or destroying irreplaceable porcelain with a pointy elbow, or permanently gouging delicate, centuries-old veneer with a hairpin.

What about the fear of fire, floods, earthquakes, volcanic eruption, leaking roofs, overflowing bathtubs, plumbing gone wrong? Or even barbarian hordes, revolution, and war? As much as she'd always admired and longed for a bit of luxury in her lifetime, this was far too much of it to be responsible for.

Just as she closed the door behind her, a woman with a vacuum cleaner materialized, and she watched Callie with far too much curiosity. *She knows you've been poking your nose into some place you shouldn't.*

"*Bonjour*," said Callie.

The woman only stared some more and didn't bother returning her greeting. Scraping a few shreds of dignity together, Callie headed down the corridor. Where was that stairway leading to the mezzanine and the servants' kitchen? Shouldn't it be straight ahead? She took a turning to the left and ended up in a dead end with a large locked wooden door in front of her. *I'll have to leave a trail of breadcrumbs each time I venture out.*

Doubling back, she returned to the stairway, and then headed back down the corridor again, closely watched by the grimly unsmiling ancestors in their gilded frames.

"You have every reason to look so glum," Callie muttered to them. "The Revolution was no fun at all, and those heavy garments and powdered wigs you're wearing don't look in the least bit comfortable."

Several wrong turnings later, she did manage to find the former refectory. Finally. She pushed open the door, stopped. The room was empty. Where was everybody? Had they all gone off on one of Nicholas' "excursions," leaving her behind because she'd risen too late? Impossible. It was only eight fifteen in the morning. Perhaps other plans had been made, plans she'd missed because she hadn't understood much of anything. *Phooey.*

In place of salads, there were other gustatory offerings: fresh baguettes, slices of cheese, a high mound of yellow butter, eggs, vegetables, also hot water for tea. Thankfully, there was a coffee machine—although this too strong, very bitter French espresso would take some getting used to. In compensation, the croissants were flaky, buttery.

Should she help herself or wait for the others? Why wait? Evidently, they preferred lolling in their beds instead of getting to work. *Those who work the hardest get where they want to go.* Besides, she was ravenously hungry. Heaping her plate high with an egg, cheeses, and thick creamy yogurt, she tucked in.

It was only when she had finished eating, that the door opened and Azeline Dubon appeared, a stack of white linens in her arms. *How stylish she is in that silk blouse and jeans. Early in the morning, and she's as chic as yesterday evening.* Hers was an inborn chic, too, for she wore no makeup and did nothing to hide the streaks of silver in her dark, curling hair.

"Good morning, Callie. Did you sleep well?"

"Very well, thank you." Although that was only partly true. It had taken her considerable time to settle down in the sumptuous bed that had to be several hundred years old. The shapes of furniture, the unusual light, the shadows that seemed to shift in the gloom, the scents of damp grass and rain drifting in from outside, all those had kept her awake long after she had turned out the light. "But where is everyone?"

"Most are in bed. When they do decide to get up, they head for the carriage house. That's where the art atelier is."

"Oh. And where's that?"

"Easy to find. When you leave this room, go down the stairs and turn right. A little further along, turn right again. The back door will be in front of you, so go outside, turn left, pass the kitchen garden, keep walking, and you'll see the carriage house. You can't miss it."

"Right." Although Callie knew she was bound to get hopelessly lost, especially with directions like those.

Artist's backpack slung over one shoulder, she went into the hallway and managed, after only three false starts, to find the back door. Pushing it open, ducking her head, she plunged into the horrifically foul weather outside.

As she splashed past the west wing, she noticed that it was very different from the rest. Obviously uninhabited, although the windows were as long and well proportioned as those in the east wing and central section, most were cobwebbed, and many had shattered panes. Woodwork was equally neglected, and a heavy studded door looked as though it had been locked for centuries. *How strange.*

Was there some mysterious, tragic, or unpleasant reason for such decrepitude? Perhaps the absentee owners of Froideval, whoever—and wherever—they might be, were indifferent to the fate of an estate they didn't occupy.

Avoiding, as best as possible, lake-sized puddles and churning seas of pale brown mud, half blinded by the driving rain, she headed beyond the plethora of stone and brick buildings—former stables, gardeners' huts, a dairy. One might once have been a brewery of some sort, another a bakery, and a long, granite structure must have been the menservants' quarters back in the days when châteaux were enterprises employing countless scores of people. Nothing, however, brought to mind a carriage house. *Any normal person would get lost in a maze like this.*

Soaked through, she finally located what had indubitably been a carriage house around a hundred years earlier. Two stories high, its substantial double doors had once admitted those capacious horse-drawn vehicles. "This place is so big and noticeable; it was almost sitting on my nose, and I still didn't see it," she complained sourly to herself.

Inside, there were the faint but unmistakable odors of oil paint, linseed oil, and turpentine—odors she loved, although she never worked in oils. In one corner of the large room, a young mustached man, one she'd seen in the winter garden the evening before, was smearing a large canvas with violent red. *A visual bloodbath,* Callie thought, but didn't say. Along the back wall, a half-twisted concoction of chicken wire slouched alongside pans, pots, and plaster-choked buckets—*possibly an art object, possibly just rubble*—she couldn't guess which. Otherwise, nothing much seemed to be going on.

A few people slumped listlessly on the room's several couches; others consulted their cell phones or tapped away on computers. No one spoke—and that was convenient. At least she didn't have to struggle to understand anything, or smile and agree even though she had no idea what the topic of conversation was.

This wasn't a propitious work atmosphere—not to her, it wasn't. *Unless I convert my work style. Start sculpting mud, or painting water.*

Pushing back her rain-drenched strands of hair, she dropped her artist's pack, made herself a fresh cup of coffee at the machine near the door, added a good dose of hot water (French coffee was strong enough to strip paint), then crossed the room and settled into a chair in a window-side nook. Now what?

Discouraged, at a loss, she sipped the hot brew and took in the scene. Only near the red-splotched canvas was there a bright spotlight, and the faint gray daylight seeping through high windows did nothing to dispel the overall gloom. Any other light came from computer screens and cell phones. Leaning back in her chair, she waited. *For what? For life to begin? The sun to shine? Nicholas to appear?* Waited some more. *For inspiration? For a reason to move? Do something!*

She put her empty coffee cup down on the floor

and opened her backpack. Pulling out her portable easel, she unfolded it, took out her drawing pad with its rough textured pages and her drawer storage box of pastels. Okay: no urban scenery, no city streets, no rough walls to draw, no roofs, no picturesque gateways.

She began sketching in gray, drawing the figures that were no more than vague shapes, mere shadows in the room's dimness. And that bright glaring spotlight! And the artificial computer beams. Defining their values, she layered, created a scene in penumbra and ambiguity. She was so absorbed in her work, she hadn't noticed that someone had come up behind her.

"Pastel? It's very strong for pastel art."

A compliment? Callie raised her head, hoping to see Nicholas. Instead, it was the mustached, blood-red-canvas man. Looking down, she inspected what she'd done, took in the sober obscurity of it. Strong? Yes, perhaps it was…in a way.

Did she like what she had produced? She didn't know. She had never drawn anything like this before. But perhaps this was the goal of the retreat. Taken out of her element, away from the familiar city streets that usually inspired her, she had stepped out of her artistic comfort zone.

"Does pastel have to be weak?" she asked.

"Of course not." Pulling up a chair, he sat down beside her. "My name is Laurent, and I consider myself a painter, nothing else. Not a conceptualist. Most people here will tell me—and you, too—that we are reactionary, using paint or pastel to express ourselves." His smile was joyless. "But we are also lucky because there is a new interest in traditional painting and sculpture. People, tired of what passes for fashionable at this time, will come to see what we, the real artists, are doing."

"I hope you're right," said Callie.

"I know I am," Laurent declared without the tiniest tinge of modesty. "Look at what the nonconceptual artists are creating, the ones who are part of the *Coopérative visuelle*."

Callie felt rather dull, for the name meant nothing to her.

"Or the others who work in this area, those whose work is incredibly forceful, for example, Marie Deluce, Elise Grondin, and MAX."

Okay, she was on safer ground now. "Yes, I know Marie Deluce's fantastic sculptures in glass, beads, and mirrors, and I've seen Elise Grondin's imaginary worlds. As for MAX—" She stopped, spread her hands. "I saw his exhibition in London. Those huge paintings of his are so forceful, I was almost intimidated."

"He's incredibly talented," Laurent agreed. "So is Elise Grondin. Did you know that she lives in a village only ten kilometers from here?"

"No, I had no idea."

"I'd love to go see her workspace. I'll ask around, see if someone can arrange a visit. As for the notoriously crowd-shy MAX..." Laurent's expression was wistful. "Maybe one day he'll let us into his atelier, too. It's such a short distance away."

"That would be quite an experience."

Laurent stood, returned to his painting. Callie stretched, then carried her drawing to the open doorway of the carriage house. Carefully, she applied the layers of fixative, so necessary for delicate work in this powdery medium that could disappear with a few unfortunate shakes of paper.

Suddenly, the hairs on the back of her neck rose. Nicholas was here, right beside her—he did have an odd way of appearing silently. He barely glanced at what she had created and made no comment. Was she hoping for approval? Perhaps only acknowledgement. What he offered was absolute indifference.

"Are you interested in going to see the exhibition at a gallery in Frieux this afternoon?" he asked.

"Oh yes!" she gushed, then, inwardly, winced. *You sound like a lovesick fan, a teenage groupie. How silly he must think you are. And how undignified.*

But his face betrayed no emotion and certainly no amusement. "We will start right after lunch."

"Great."

He moved away with that stealthy, sleek male strut. Carefully, Callie slipped her finished piece into her sketchbook, and then covered it with protective tissue.

So Nicholas had pointedly ignored her work. She should be feeling wounded, or even offended, but she didn't. Why? Because she knew that men like Nicholas Trier didn't tread into other people's courtyards; they expected everyone to flock to theirs.

For now, she would concentrate on the one important thing that had happened: she, of all the others, had been singled out for an outing with Nicholas Trier. Wasn't that something? She could almost hear the witty and intelligent conversation they were bound to have. Despite all the discouraging rain, what an unusually lucky day this was turning out to be.

****

Except it wasn't. She hadn't received any special treatment. She was merely one of a gaggle of nine—the two cooing arm-hangers included—who piled into two cars and headed down toward the main road. At least, relegated to a back seat, she didn't need to take part in the conversation that swirled around her in the usual high-pitched incomprehensible way.

The gallery, another one of those new buildings in glass, concrete, and metal, was indubitably the pride and joy of the small city of Frieux, and like a clutch of ducklings trailing behind a solicitous papa duck, all followed Nicholas as he led them up a flight of stairs to the main exhibition space.

Silently, all listened assiduously to his words, bobbed their heads when he analyzed art works that consisted of random numbers embossed on chunks of slate, abstract fuzzy photos, and a collection of unrelated objects. One piece, entitled "Afternoon Contemplation," consisted of six glasses of water placed on a high shelf.

Callie thought, only briefly, that she should make an effort, try to appreciate the intellectual convolutions that resulted in such…representations…but she was ineluctably indifferent. Time trickled on, as slow as cold molasses. How long could she trudge along, play at being a cohesive sycophant?

She lagged farther and farther behind until all had turned a corner and were out of sight. Relieved to be alone, she began exploring other sections of the amazingly large gallery. To her delight, she found a room filled with paintings. Here were landscapes, portraits, and blazes of color. Some were abstract, others figurative, and Callie was pleased to be getting her teeth into something that excited her. Not theories, not words.

Half an hour later, she found the others gathered near the front door. No one mentioned her absence— had they noticed she'd been gone? Probably not. They'd been too intent on listening to Nicholas, absorbing his every word. *Demonstrating how seriously they take the art world and his lofty place in it.*

However, Nicholas hadn't been fooled. One questioning eyebrow raised, he watched her approach, yet made no comment, not in front of everyone else. Why? *Because he might lose face.*

Yes…she truly understood how men like Nicholas functioned. *They bask in the role of leading man. They demand unlimited loyalty and attention; they need admiration and constant reassurance.* But when someone resisted, even a little, that person would be singled out for special attention.

Her ex-husband, Malcolm, had been a man of the same ilk. In the beginning of their relationship, he'd been enamored of her, mainly because she hadn't joined the bevy of art students who'd succumbed to his astonishing charm. He'd had to work hard at winning her over. It was only later, once they were married, that she'd made the fatal mistake of giving up her own artistic career to promote his.

She was older and much wiser now. She knew she didn't have to give up her view of art; she didn't have to demonstrate loyalty to Nicholas. She was aware that he was interested, even intrigued, by her. *All I have to do is wait patiently. Surely, he'll make the first move.*

Chapter Six

The following morning brought the usual leaden sky and buffeting wind, but at least it wasn't raining. Distant hills were mist-shrouded; hedgerows shivered, and grass lay flat and soggy.

Taking in the scene from her bedroom window, Callie wondered for the umpteenth time what she'd let herself in for. All she could see were trees, more trees, hedges, then more hedges. *That's not a happy place out there.*

It wasn't because she feared the creepy crawlies that lurked in vegetation, or because slimy creatures snuggled under every fluttering leaf—she'd always found wild animals and insects rather cute. As a child, she'd counted on dung beetles, ladybugs, caterpillars, bees, snails, slugs, wasps, foxes, rabbits, stoats, crows, and hedgehogs for friendship.

But she'd never fully digested the two years when her mother, after joining yet another esoteric cult—one run by a wall-eyed, skinny man—decided that life in a homemade twig teepee would be an idyllic one. For mind-numbing hours each day, cult members had drummed, chanted in a grotesque, secret language, assumed strange and uncomfortable praying postures, and hoped to contact a long-dead Egyptian seer.

If that hadn't been awful enough, teepee life in Northern England had had little to recommend it. In icy winter, food and water had frozen solid, toes and fingers burned with cold, and in her cheap and nasty sleeping bag, Callie had shivered away the endless miserable nights. *And now, here I am. Stuck in the backwoods again.*

She could do three things. One: pack up her belongings, head for the train station, and chug back to London. Two: spend another day in the carriage house drawing shadows in artificial computer light. Three: head out into that agrarian salad just outside her window. *Yuck.*

Okay, she was no coward. Why let her long-dead mother's bad choices ruin these two weeks at the château? When this retreat ended, she was planning to take the train to Paris, then spend one whole week going to museums, hearing inspired conversations in cafés, and relishing the noise, the polluted air, the snarled traffic, the conmen, the muggers, and the pickpockets. She was looking forward to all of it.

But before those pleasurable days came around, there was this…countryside…to contend with. Groaning, she slipped into a pair of jeans, pulled on her practical walking boots, and a windbreaker. Then grabbing her backpack, she headed for the servants' kitchen.

Louis, the silver-haired server she had met in the winter garden on her first evening in Froideval, was standing near the buffet table and sipping a coffee. Noticing the backpack, he raised one eyebrow. "Are you heading out into the wild?"

"Risking my skin," Callie joked and hoped he couldn't detect her lack of exuberance.

He smiled. "Since you're planning to work outside,

this is your lucky day. There won't be any rain for a change—or so the often-untruthful weather lady has promised us. Why don't you pack up enough food for a picnic? That way, if you find a pleasant place to stay, you won't have to come back here when you're hungry."

"Good idea," said Callie. She was lying through her teeth, but why offend Louis? He seemed such a kindly man, she didn't dare tell him that she had no intention of tramping over squishy grass all day but planned to get back here as quickly as possible. However, since he was standing close by, she felt obliged to play along. She selected an apple, bread, cucumber slices, tomatoes, and enough cheese for a satisfying sandwich, wrapped all in a large table napkin, and headed out.

Leaving by the back door, she passed the raised beds of the kitchen garden where, this morning, a divine, wild-haired young woman was kneeling in the mocha brown dirt and tending to what might be early lettuces and radishes. *And ruining her fingernails, too.*

The woman looked up. "*Bonjour*," she called cheerily and waved a tiny trowel.

"*Bonjour*," Callie answered and wondered how anyone digging holes in muck could sound so chirpy.

A narrow, unpaved lane led through the dripping, luxuriant green, and she followed it, fighting her way through mud and spongy weeds, while clusters of curious magpies sent their noisy approbation into the damp air. They were instantly challenged by a far more cacophonous pair of jays. On the distant hills, a few lonely granite farmhouses perched, but there didn't seem to be a soul around anywhere, and only the faint barking of dogs suggested that, somewhere, humans might be present. *Or ogres, or mad cult leaders, or the Jolly Green Giant.*

She reached a narrow slice of valley, where wind was softened to a tickling breeze. The earthy scent was intense, and wildflowers—vetch, old man's beard, wild carrot—nodded their late spring welcome. And beyond an outcrop of rock, a limpid olive-green pond promised a happy haven for frogs.

Okay, she had to admit it: it was a pretty scene, a peaceful one. What if she stayed here for a little while? *And do what? Draw scenery? Yuck.* Didn't millions of people paint, draw, and photograph such scenes all the time? *So what? Why not—just as an exercise—draw it now?*

She settled down on the flattest part of the rock, and it was just as cold, hard, humid, and uncomfortable as she feared it would be: *Thank you, Nature.* Opening her backpack, she pulled out her small storage box with its drawers of pastel crayons and settled her sketchpad on her knees.

Feeling unreservedly disconsolate, with herself, with her clammy socks and shoes, with the dank vegetable kingdom surrounding her, and with her own ambitions, she began sketching, rubbing, and blending. And, covering page after page, she tried to drum up interest in what she was doing, find the thrill of starting a new project.

Suddenly, she thought she heard something—an unusual noise. What was it? Listening, she waited, tense and wary. She was not a fearful or skittish woman, and the noise was hardly threatening, yet this was an isolated place in an unfamiliar country—anyone would be uneasy.

As she looked over at the green path on her left, a horse appeared, shaggy-footed, and uncommonly large. A wooden cart followed, rumbling along the uneven trail, and it was loaded with bushy trees. A moving forest? *Am I imagining things? Is Great Birnham Wood coming to high Dunsinane Hill?* Of course it wasn't. Macbeth was long gone; neither Birnham Wood nor Dunsinane Hill, wherever they might once have been, were anywhere near rural France. *Furthermore, this is real life, not a play written by Shakespeare. So perhaps I've been dropped into a time warp, entered another century, headed out on a different life story?*

A man emerged next, and beside him was a large and bounding multicolored dog of indeterminate breed. Catching sight of her, the man stopped and smiled. Relieved, she let out her breath. It was Michel Alexandre.

"Hello," he called.

She smiled back at him. "Nice to see you again." It was.

"Foumi," he called to the horse. "Halt."

The old cart clattered to a stop. Michel went over to the horse, affectionately patted its brown flank. Then, accompanied by the strange-looking dog, he sauntered over the grassy knoll and came to the rock where she was sitting.

Wagging its rather seedy tail, the dog scrutinized her. It seemed a mild enough creature, nothing to be afraid of, although she knew nothing about dogs, about pets of any variety. Tentatively, she reached out, let the beast sniff her hand, then she patted its head. The raggedly tail swung with increased confidence.

"I'm surprised to find you here," said Michel.

"What's so surprising?" Had he sensed her dislike of the rural world when they'd first met?

"You've wandered some distance away from Froideval. The artists who come there usually stay within the grounds."

It was what she'd intended to do…at first. But why let him know he'd touched a sore spot? She looked over at the hairy-footed horse and old wooden cart. "I think it's a lot more surprising to find someone wandering through the countryside with a horse and wagon. What happened to that battered old van of yours? Did it finally give up the ghost?"

He glared, but the impish glow in his deep brown eyes told her he wasn't offended. "Battered old van you call it? Don't you know a collector's item—a prized antique car—when you see it?"

He had to be joking, didn't he? "It's an antique? No, I guess I don't."

"It's a Citroen H *utilitaire*. Born in 1955. It still has its original motor, and there's no corrosion." He seemed to be very proud of his wreck. "Besides, keeping an old car, making sure it passes the pollution tests, is more ecologically responsible than buying a new car."

"I suppose so," said Callie, who thought, but didn't dare say, that perhaps the comforts of modernity should also be taken into consideration.

Michel settled down on the rock near her. "And, to answer your question, coming to work with a horse and wagon is less polluting than a car."

"Fine. Horses don't guzzle gas, fill the air with carbon emissions, or contribute significantly to climate change."

"And I can guarantee that Foumi doesn't have an internal combustion engine."

"Neither do electric cars," she said triumphantly.

"Except the production and disposal of electric cars is less environmentally friendly than processing internal combustion cars."

She squinted at him. "Are you another one of those people with an answer for everything?" Why did she feel vaguely miffed?

"No." He waved a dismissing hand. "Not everything. But I do defend what I know is right. And, in this case, that means going about my job with a horse and cart wins out every time. Why? Because horses crop their hay and grasses in areas often useless to agriculture. Also, they aren't noisy, they don't use fuel, they don't need expensive repairs, and they're financially more viable than cars. Even better, unlike cars, horses don't kill a horrific number of animals, insects, reptiles, birds, and other humans each year."

"You certainly don't have any problem finding a parking space," chirped Callie, deciding that agreement was easier than resistance. "And a horse will take you places where no car can go."

"All true." Michel examined the waiting horse with unmistakable tenderness. "That being said, I don't ever get into the cart and let Foumi pull me. She's an old girl, and I want to keep her in excellent shape, just so I can have her company for as long as possible."

"Sounds good to me, although I know nothing about having a horse for company."

"It doesn't have to be a horse. Any animal—a dog, a horse, a pig, a chicken, or a rat—gives us a connection to nature and a feeling of peace. Animals are also aesthetically pleasing."

Callie couldn't help sizing up the huge dog now seated comfortably beside her. Grayish, brownish, partially spotted with white, it was a long, thin-nosed, bristly creature with floppy, lily-pad ears. No one in the whole world could ever call it visually attractive or graceful. Or pretty.

Catching her glance, Michel snorted. "Romeo can't help the way he looks. His mother wasn't choosy when it came to partners."

"Romeo? That's his name? And he's no breed at all?"

"Pure animal rescue." Fondly, he eyed the grazing horse. "Like Foumi over there who was tied up in a field and left to die."

"How horrible." Callie reached out, stroked Romeo's head again. His fur was unexpectedly soft despite its scratchy appearance. "I'll never understand cruelty to animals, although I wasn't allowed to own a dog, or a cat, or even a hamster when I was growing up. Not that I didn't want a pet."

"Your parents didn't like animals?"

"Parent—singular. No father that I know of. With my mother, I led an itinerant life. There was no money left over to feed a pet and no settled home for very long."

"Doesn't sound very easy."

She wondered why she'd even mentioned her childhood. It wasn't a subject she liked talking about, and she hated people feeling sorry for her. "On the positive side, because my mother's gift for home schooling was pretty close to null, I kept myself happy by drawing. At least she always supplied me with wax crayons."

"And from there, you graduated to pastel."

"Right." She waited for him to criticize her choice of medium, tell her she was out of fashion. He didn't.

"Can I see some of your work?"

She quailed. "I'm afraid I haven't done anything that I'm very proud of today. Just flowers and trees, and landscape. All of it looks so bland, so...unremarkable." Embarrassed, she opened her drawing pad, handed it to him, then waited silently while he turned the pages, his face expressionless.

"Pastels are a good choice for you," he said, finally. "You have a knack for capturing light, and you use shadow in a very clever way."

Callie gaped, wide-eyed. The last thing she had expected was encouragement. "But there's nothing going on in those drawings. They're boring. There's nothing startling, nothing satisfying."

"What would satisfy you?"

"I wish I knew." She flapped her hands in discouragement. "I'm pretty sure that just doing pretty pictures with flowers would drive me crazy in very little time. I'm not the sort of person who appreciates nature, or fields, or being in the country." She stopped. Should she have admitted that to a man who spent his life working with greenery? Possibly not. It made her sound so...snobbish. "I know that must sound silly to you, but being outside in a field really isn't my favorite thing. I prefer cities."

"Some people do," said Michel, mildly. His eyes were as friendly as usual, therefore he was not offended by her declaration. "So you're not satisfied with what you've been drawing today. Fine. Have you worked on anything else since coming here?"

She felt incredibly uncomfortable for some reason. "Well…yesterday morning I did one pastel that I think I like. That looks like something. It was raining, you see, and there I was, sitting in the carriage house at Froideval, doubting that I'd ever see the sun again, wondering what I was doing here in France, and deciding I probably wasn't meant to be an artist. And because I was weary and discouraged, I took out my pastels and drew what I saw around me."

"Do you have the drawing here?"

She took a deep breath. Did she want to show him what she'd done? Why not? Pulling out her other, larger sketchbook, she opened it and lifted the protecting cellophane covering the somber work.

Michel studied it for a long minute. Then smiled. "Excellent."

"It is? You sincerely think so?"

"You know it is. That's why you like it. That's why you're proud of it."

"Maybe. But I haven't done anything decent since then. All I've portrayed is prettiness."

"It's a question of light, of course."

"Light?"

"As you know, with pastels, there are only two options. You can start with dark paper as a background, then draw in the light, underline it with color, and let the paper predominate, as Millet and Dégas did. Or you can start with light paper, add in the shadows, just the way you have in this interior."

"In other words, I should keep on drawing interiors?"

"Only if you want to. But, in my opinion,

satisfaction comes through experimenting. You have to challenge yourself, feel so uncomfortable that you can't be happy until you discover your unique style."

If I have one. But she understood what he meant. All she'd been doing for years was reproducing what she'd always done—houses, walls, streets, buildings. Sticking to safe ground and to a known technique. Taking the easy way, never risking failure. But if she didn't change all that, she'd just go on feeling bored.

Michel stood, brushed the seat of his trousers, glanced at the cart, at Foumi who was still ripping up grassy shoots and grinding them into mush with apparent delectation. "Try to keep one thing in mind: what you don't draw is far more important than what you do draw."

Confused, she peered up at him. "Meaning?"

With wide-open arms, he took in the whole swath of countryside. "Look at this sky. Dull, flat, gray. But gray skies reveal far more than bright sun. Sun bleaches out colors, but look how many greens you can see on a day like this. Look at the intensity of yellow and pink flowers. In such flat light, you see every detail of every plant, every blade of grass, every hair on a nettle, and every rib on every leaf. But you can't—and you shouldn't—depict all of that. You have to make choices. Eliminate. Concentrate."

Then, dogged by tail-wagging Romeo, Michel turned, crossed back over the knoll, and waved goodbye. Minutes later, man, dog, horse, and ancient cart were out of view...then out of sound. Leaving behind the peace and quiet, the birdsong, the buzzing of insects, and the rustling noises of busy creatures in the humid vegetation.

Make choices. What you leave out is more important than what you do. It was all so confusing…or was it? Perhaps he had given her an important key.

But wasn't it odd that Michel Alexandre, an amateur artist, a struggler like herself, had been the first and only person to take an interest in her work? To have, perhaps, set her off on a quest? Presented her with a challenge? *But what if you end up in another dead end?* She smiled to herself. Wasn't that what taking risks was all about?

Chapter Seven

Although the air was as damp as the interior of a wet sponge, the evening was sweet smelling and mild. After dinner, the artists lolled in the wrought iron chairs under the ancient oaks at the side of the château.

As usual, the discussions about art were fervent, and although Callie envied their ease in repartee, she was grateful that her limited fluency did give her a good excuse for remaining on the outside of the general clamor. She'd always preferred being an observer.

And, as such, she watched Nicholas Trier. He was flanked, as usual, by the full-lipped blonde whose name, Callie now knew, was Katell, and by Pascale, the sexy brunette. Long and lean, Nicholas sprawled casually on a garden chair, his legs stretched out in front of him and crossed at the ankle, and his knowing half smile acknowledged the respect, even awe, that he garnered from all. Yes, he knew how to make use of his superior position. Before he spoke, he waited—even insisted—on absolute silence; when contradicted, he ignored the argument.

Callie couldn't help remembering the other beautiful men she'd known—and hastily discarded: Pete, the rusty-haired Australian with delphinium eyes. After his dinner invitation to an expensive and trendy bistro, he had, with a divine ripple of muscular shoulders, declared himself skint. And Callie understood that this was how he negotiated the social world: collecting drooling women who happily pulled out their credit cards. After Pete, there had been sleek Randy who survived on high-protein smoothies. He'd jawed on without pause about vital body functions, techniques for building muscle and bone, for regulating acid-base balance, and had shared, at great length, his personal tips for increasing immunity to disease.

Only once had Callie managed to change the subject, asking him what sort of art he liked (she didn't dare bring up the subject of literature). He'd taken a long sip of his coconut-flake chocolate-flavored multi-protein power smoothie and in a manner suggesting superior wisdom, had announced he was too busy to spend time examining people's scribbles.

But Nicholas was different. Although he shared the physical excellence of men such as Pete and Randy (and, of course, Malcolm), he was an intellectual. And a success. A man who could—if she played her cards right—take her where she wanted to go in the art world.

Art? What were they all talking about now? Praising the work of an artist whose exhibition had consisted of two hundred and fifty restaurant menus collected from all over the country, then glued on to thick squares of vinyl. Tiny accompanying maps had shown where each restaurant was located.

"Why," Callie muttered, "is this art? Why would anyone be interested in going to see it?" She was so obviously out of tune.

There was silence. Yes, she had spoken out loud, putting her foot in her mouth, as she too often did. Saying the wrong things, to the wrong people, at the wrong times. Being honest instead of discreet, or even hypocritical. Offending those she shouldn't, yet always going out of her way to apologize to lampposts when she walked into them, or steering cranky old folk across busy streets when all they wanted was to be left alone, or making sure she walked elsewhere instead of squashing underfoot a long line of busy worker ants.

And if the looks people were shooting her way weren't fully hostile, they weren't friendly either.

"You said?" Katell eyed her with overt scorn.

Callie met the scorn head-on; she wasn't easily intimidated. "Just making general conversation. You're quite welcome to participate." Then, inwardly, she crowed with satisfaction. This time, at least, her grammar hadn't abandoned her.

Katell turned away. *Cat's got her tongue.* But Ottilie, a petite woman with intense eyes and carroty hair, chirped, "Conceptual art is a valid contribution to the normative caesura in the history of art."

At least that was what Callie *thought* the woman had said. She wondered if, had her French been fluent, she'd heard a valid argument or sheer incomprehensible mumbo jumbo.

A few of the others murmured their approval, so it must have meant something to some of them.

Another woman, Geraldine, was more kindly. "If it hadn't been for the advent of conceptual art in the 1960s, many of us would never have become artists. In the other movements, you had to define yourself by medium. Conceptual art democratized art practices."

Callie said nothing further. What could she possibly contribute? This was definitely not the hill she wanted to die on.

Nicholas, head tilted back and eyes half-lidded,

was watching her with undisguised amusement. "Do you have difficulty understanding what we're saying, Callie? After all, this isn't your language."

There was something else in his tone...what? Ridicule? Why had he singled her out like this? Because he had resented her question? She felt like a rather dull schoolgirl, the one person in the class who didn't know the right answer.

"Yes, I do sometimes have trouble following the conversation," she admitted, although she knew she was being patronized.

Nicholas bobbed his head, rather like a sage. "The conceptual gesture is the recourse of fully aware artists working in the current historical condition of art production."

Was this a rebuke or a criticism? Or more cant. She was annoyed but pushed the emotion down. She forced herself to stay seated, although she would have much preferred to leave the group, stride out into the park's deep shadows where trees were cottony forms against a summer night's milky sky, where stars punched through the heavens like twinkling Christmas lights.

The discussion continued, and her thoughts wandered. Michel's words came back to her: "Bring lightness into dark. Choose what to depict. Eliminate detail and become precise." Okay then, what if she tried sketching in the spaces between branches instead of the branches themselves? Or if she merely suggested the tufting grasses close to the ground. *Why not draw the invisible?* She smiled, mocking herself and her silly ideas.

Laurent, his knuckles bearing traces of the blood-red paint he used, sat down on the chair beside hers.

"You've been gone all day, and you're lucky, because you've escaped all the pompous discourse," he murmured. "Everybody here has been rattling on endlessly about the same things. Roger, that curly-haired man sitting over by the hedge, told us that if we aren't into minimal artistic expression, there's no point in doing anything at all. Sandrine, that pretty dark-haired girl, was furious. Like you and me, she uses more traditional techniques, weaves cloths and string with wire, and creates figurative scenes in a very original way. You should have heard her go at Roger, hammer and tongs."

"Aside from you, do the other people get any work done here?" Callie asked.

"Some. Most are here to make contact and stimulate each other. Like musicians, writers, and dancers, we artists occupy a marginal position in society, and that's a good reason for us to stick together."

Except, thought Callie, the only real stimulation she had received so far was from an amateur, possibly mediocre, painter who had nothing to do with the château…aside from being a gardener on its grounds.

****

It was as black as India ink when she woke. What time was it? Two or three in the morning? What had jolted her out of the world of dreams? Lying still, she strained to hear. Was someone whispering out in the hallway? What was going on? Slipping out of her warm bed, she tiptoed to her bedroom door. Opened it slowly. And saw it.

A ghost, pale, stealthy, yet strangely substantial, was flitting through the far end of the corridor. Her heart pounding wildly, Callie squinted and tried to grasp what was reality, or what might be, without doubt, the juicy fruit of uncontrolled imagination.

Then she almost giggled. Despite being faintly illuminated by one small nightlight only, it was easy to see that the ghost was very human, and that it wore a silvery dressing gown. Which human it was, she couldn't tell. Fair hair, tall. A man. Was it Nicholas or one of the male artists? The figure slipped into a room at the end of the hall. *Musical beds*. She only wondered who was indulging.

****

After lunch the next day, she took Nicholas up on the offer to visit his studio on the second floor of the gatehouse. It wasn't a personal invitation: Colette was here, too, standing beside Roger. Sandrine and a few of the others were equally present. And it was an attractive workspace. The large skylight faced north, and time had polished the planked floor into a coppery glow. But there were things she missed: the pungent smells of the paints and materials that marked out an artist's world. There were no stacked canvases; there was no chaos. *Of course there wouldn't be. This is only a temporary studio. Nicholas' real life is in Paris. But still…*

Callie thought of her own tiny workspace in London, in a building that had, in another century, been a posh family townhouse. Near the one large window, there was an easel, a table with trays of pastel crayons. Below, sheaves of paper were stacked neatly. And on a rather rickety bookshelf, art books were piled high. Yet, as minuscule as that mini-atelier was, it implied work, and a devotion to art.

Here, in Nicholas' studio, walls were stark and

white. Aside from framed pictures of calligraphic Japanese ideograms, there was little of visual interest. On one long table were two computers, several screens, and a confusion of electronic drawing tablets.

It was a strangely sterile artist's studio. *Anyway, for me, it's sterile. For Nicholas, it's unquestionably the sort of emptiness he needs for his work—those large words and letters combined with enigmatic sayings.*

Her thoughts were interrupted by Gregory, frizzy-haired and aggressive. Fingers snapping, arms windmilling, he stood in the middle of the room and held forth with bellicose conviction: "Any work of art more than twenty years old should be removed from the museums. Paintings and sculptures are outdated. Art has to reflect society as it is now, as it will be in the future. We artists are visionaries."

Irritated, Callie moved to the far corner where another vigorous debate was taking place.

"Paris is the only place to be. It is the nerve center of France! How can an artist be effective when living far from the very cradle of intellectual thought?"

"What do you mean? In Paris there are so many artists per square kilometer, you get lost in the crush."

Not the center of attention, Nicolas Trier stretched out indolently in a very contemporary sling chair. He wasn't participating, just listening to the conversation, and smiling as enigmatically as usual.

"I'll be going to Paris when this retreat ends," said Callie to no one in particular. "I'm looking forward to it."

Roger turned to her. "And I suppose you'll sit in cafés hoping to hear stimulating intellectual discussions about literature, philosophy, and art."

Deep inside, Callie winced. Yes, that was what she had in mind. "And?"

He snickered, but not unkindly. "Believe me, that's another misconception that foreigners have about France. Today, in cafés, people talk about work, or pop songs, or makeup, or clothes, or football."

Was he right? Yes, he might well be. "How very disappointing. Perhaps it's not really my century."

Just then, the door opened, and Laurent burst into the studio, his eyes dancing with excitement. He came over to where Callie was standing. "Guess what! We've been invited to Elise Grondin's atelier the day after tomorrow. We'll take several cars, so there will be room for everyone who wants to come."

"That's lovely news."

"She's expecting us in the morning, so we'll start out right after breakfast." Grinning widely, Laurent paused dramatically before continuing. "I have another surprise, too. I told Azeline that we'd like to see MAX's atelier, and she promised to organize that for us."

"Really?" How, Callie wondered, could Azeline arrange such a thing? But before she could ask, Nicholas had cut into the conversation.

"There's hardly time for so many excursions, especially since you, Callie, won't be in the country for very long. There's so much to discuss and to work out first. Besides, we're traveling to Erblon to see some valuable nineteenth-century etchings in a few days, and all of us will be attending the very important opening exhibition in the new museum in Grenache."

Callie observed him. Ever reclining in that saddle chair, he was smiling, but without mirth. What else did she see in his face? Wariness? Perhaps sheer irritation. True, Nicholas would never appreciate the work of artists like MAX or Elise Grondin, but did he resent it when those in this chosen circle did? Why would he? Artists weren't rivals. They worked in different ways, had different goals.

If she hoped for a clue, it wasn't forthcoming. He cleverly steered the conversation away from local artists and onto the architectural merits of the museum in Grenache, where he and the others in the forefront of the contemporary scene would be participating in that prestigious show.

****

Late that night, the ghosts were at it again. She'd gone into the hallway for a trip down to the bathroom when she saw a head poke out of a doorway—quite a different doorway from the other night—then jerk back. A door clicked shut.

Did someone want to slip into a room without being seen? Or perhaps people were spying on each other. *If only I knew who slept where. Perhaps if I watch more closely during the day, I'll pick up a few telltale clues.* But even if she did, what did that matter? She yawned. *Now if I had a French lover, my vocabulary would certainly improve, but I bet my shaky syntax would go straight to hell.*

Chapter Eight

In the morning, she set out with her backpack, took the same grassy lane, passed shady vales where bluebells hung their shy heads, skirted a field where three woolly sheep stood belly-deep in blazing yellow, purple, and pink. On either side, wild weeds and brambles formed riotous hedges, and over their bushy tips, she could see the oddly shaped fields beyond.

The sun had made a rare but shy appearance from behind a bank of cloud, and its rays were touching the countryside with a tender light. She stopped, contemplated the scene. *Time I started appreciating where I've landed. Didn't I come here to change my outlook? Challenge narrow ideas?* Hadn't she been dragging her dislike of the countryside around for long enough? She wasn't a child anymore. She was close to fifty.

Reaching the same sweet scoop of valley where she had spent the day drawing, she again made herself as comfortable as possible on the chunk of gray rock. Again she took out paper and pastels, waited, and hesitated. Right over there were bright flowers and proud trees. Beyond, the hesitant blue horizon was scratched by shaggy hills, and such a scene begged to be drawn. So did the swoop of daisy-rich meadows. But she resisted the lure of all.

She would try doing as Michel had suggested:

select, eliminate, remove, mute, and then see how far such visual abstinence would take her. Concentrating on the shaded spaces between the blades of grass and the undersides of leaves, she sketched, smudged, and started again. It was laborious work, teaching herself a new way of functioning and, hours later, she wasn't satisfied with the result. But not entirely dissatisfied either.

Thinking hard, tapping a pencil against her lower lip, she thought of Michel, his horse, and his cart filled with shrubs. Wouldn't it be nice to see him? Talk with him? She had hoped he would pass by, but he hadn't. She could always go search for the man, but how, in this vast rolling countryside, would she find him?

Hadn't he said he was rewilding the area? Hadn't his cart been filled with bushy things? Planting trees was a slow enough business, so he couldn't be very far off, could he? She hoped not. Perhaps all she had to do was follow the track he had taken when she'd last seen him.

Packing her supplies into her backpack, she stood and headed out. It wasn't easy going. After all the recent rainfall, the ground was sludgy and slippery, and sinking into deep puddles, she thoroughly soaked both boots and socks. *Now I know exactly why I hate the natural world.* Yet on she went. He had to be out here somewhere. And why was it so important to find him? Because conversation with him was rewarding—far more so than the daily debates at the retreat.

Soon enough, just around a bend in the lane, she caught sight of the cart. A few paces away, Foumi, unhitched from the vehicle, was ripping up grass shoots with epicurean lust. But it was Romeo who came bounding over to her, barking elatedly and wagging his scrubby tail as if she were a long lost but very dear friend.

Twenty feet away, there was Michel, kneeling on the dark, dank earth, as if that was the best place in the world to be. Beside him lay a small spade and a piled tangle of young green saplings.

"Hi," she called and then wondered if he would consider her arrival an intrusion. He'd stated he was a lone wolf on the day they'd met, had told her he took pleasure in solitude. Now here she was, invading this space where he'd been working peacefully. Bringing chatter into a place where the only sounds had been birdsong, Foumi's chomping, and Romeo's grunts of pleasure as he rolled on the ground. But, coming closer, she saw Michel was smiling, and that was a relief.

"Hi, yourself," he answered.

She was standing only a few feet away from him now. "What are you planting?" Not that his answer would mean anything to her.

"As it happens, I'm replanting, although it's rather late in the season to be doing this. I'm hoping that all the recent rain will help these little shrubs to take root and grow back into a healthy hedge."

She scanned the lumpy stretch of ground in the otherwise featureless field. A long line up of scraggly twigs had been freshly slotted into place, but they looked almost too flimsy to survive. "Because there was a full hedge here before?"

"Yes. For over eight hundred years, there was. A hedgerow of brambles, ivy, shrubs, clematis, oak trees, hazel trees, and flowering plants. And it provided a healthy, balanced environment for many creatures—

dormice, birds, toads, snakes, also invertebrates like beetles, snails, and butterflies."

Callie dropped her backpack and, uninvited, sat down on the soggy ground not far from where he was digging. She didn't even own a houseplant, but a banal, normal conversation about twigs, saplings, and small creatures was what she craved at the moment. "Okay, even I know that hedgerows contain more flowering plants than forests."

His left eyebrow quirked. "Strange thing for a city girl to know. Especially one who told me that she isn't fond of the countryside."

"Look, I'm naturally more comfortable in cities, that's all I meant. I suppose I overreact to being in the country because of those itinerant childhood years I think I mentioned." She flipped one hand dismissively. No way did she want to talk about her tawdry upbringing. "Go on, tell me more. Why isn't there a hedge here now?"

"Because some thirty years ago, the farmer who worked these lands belonging to Froideval ripped out the hedges in order to have larger fields for his agricultural machinery. Now we're trying to bring back that balanced environment." He pointed to the rolling hills. "You see those uplands? They look pretty from here, gentle, lush, and green. But when you go up to them and take a closer look, you realize that they're bleak, overgrazed, chemically sterile, and devoid of diverse natural life."

"You're not planning to replace every single lost hedge on your own, are you?"

"Of course not," he scoffed. Picking up the small spade, he loosened another patch of earth. "There are thousands of trees and shrubs to replant, and that would be an impossible task for only one person. I'm part of a group of volunteers, and so far we've covered many kilometers. There are other volunteers, too, people who fight against irresponsible agricultural practices, habitat destruction, and factory farming."

With gentle fingers, he spread the delicate roots of a tiny shrub, tucked it into place in the little hole, then tamped down the moist soil with his palm. Reached for another, and then another.

She watched silently as he planted, and strangely enough, it was almost a sensual sight. His hands were broad, strong, and deeply tanned from working outdoors; his long fingers were beautifully shaped. And under that denim shirt of his, there was the alluring suggestion of tight sinew and warm, fragrant skin. Bear like? No, not exactly. Something more, something…

"A penny for your thoughts." Michel was watching her with those disconcerting eyes of his, very dark, with heavy lids and thick lashes.

She felt the blush as it traveled upward, flooding her neck, her face. He hadn't caught what she had been thinking, had he? Perhaps he had. Surely, he'd seen how her gaze had traveled over his hands, his arms, his chest, and shoulders. How incredibly humiliating! What vaguely plausible answer could she give? "Oh…just remembering something."

"Ah." Eyebrows raised in overt amusement, he smirked—rather cockily—then went back to working on the next hole, the next shrub.

Squirming inwardly with embarrassment, Callie searched for an impersonal subject of conversation. "You really enjoy doing this work." It sounded silly enough to her own ears.

"I do. My greatest pleasures in life are bringing threatened species back from the brink, helping overgrazed knolls turn into fertile meadows, and spotting weasels, badgers, and endangered birds like skylarks, pipits, or linnets." With one soil-stained finger, he indicated a cluster of trees a short distance away. "You see that copse? Those nettles growing all around the fringe are a hotspot for butterflies and spiders. I often sneak over and spy on them."

"An agrarian voyeur," Callie teased.

He sent her a lazy smile then, with the sweetest delicacy, picked up a long pink-brown earthworm and placed it under a pile of leaves, safe from his tiny spade's silver blade.

"And you're going to tell me that earthworms are also an endangered species?"

"You'd be surprised. The earthworm population has fallen by about a third in the past twenty-five years because of extensive drainage, pesticide use, inorganic fertilizers, deep plowing, and the growing levels of animal-wormer that's being stocked in the soil."

She could feel the damp penetrate through her jeans—*the sopping wet pants look. How rustic*. But she didn't feel like leaving. It was so glorious being here, listening to him. He had a wealth of information at his fingertips, and—if you liked the color green—the surroundings were phenomenal. She took in the grasses swaying in the gentle breeze, the more stalwart reeds poking up from a nearby ditch, the pale, blue sky with its doodles of puffy cloud, the shady, secret woods beyond. "It's so peaceful. A peaceful part of the world."

His brow furrowed. "You think so?"

"Aside from all the creatures that hunt others for food."

"It wasn't always so," he said.

"I suppose not." How she liked his deep drawl, the hint of joy that seemed to hide behind every word. Raising her hand, she slowly caressed the tips of long grasses with her palm. Then saw that Michel was watching her with an unreadable expression. She dropped her hand into her lap. "The other day, Azeline told me that Froideval was originally a defense castle."

"Yes, it was."

"Tell me more." Best to keep conversation on neutral ground—if war could be considered a neutral subject.

"Think about the noble warlords who once owned Froideval. They used to send their peasants and serfs out to massacre the peasants and serfs who belonged to warlords in the surrounding castles. Why? Because, for them it was a show of power, a mere sport, a life-sized game of chess. Then, later, in the fourteenth and fifteenth centuries, the Hundred Years' War was fought here, and in the nineteenth, the Franco-Prussian War. WWI's trenches aren't far away, and tanks rolled through this countryside during WWII. Today, we're at peace in this country, but who knows how long it will last?"

"Yet you keep on planting."

"Call it optimism, if you'd like." The good-natured laugh lines deepened. "Or a love of beauty."

Yes, that was it! And what a lovely man he was! Planting, knowing each shrub would grow and become a leafy haven. It seemed such a worthy thing to do. "Can I do one?" Where did those words come from?

Michel gawped at her. He was probably as startled as she was. "You'll get your hands dirty."

"Big deal. It's only earth." My goodness. She certainly was plunging in headfirst.

With the faintest odd look, he picked up a spiny little thing and handed it to her. "*Épine noire*."

"What's special about it?"

"It's also called *prunellier*. It's a member of the rose family, a natural hedgerow plant. It produces blue berries that are too sour to enjoy. But if you put them in strong alcohol, add a good dose of sugar, then let them macerate, you end up with a nice, tangy liqueur. In the winter, when there's little else to eat, the birds thrive on the berries."

"I know! I just remembered what they are. We call them sloes in England." Spreading the roots as he had done, she put the blackthorn sprig in place and tamped down the soil—black, moist, and pleasant to the touch. Then she looked at Michel and grinned with a strange feeling of satisfaction. He grinned back. *Pure complicity*. The thought warmed her through and through.

She stayed with him until all the saplings were planted. Standing, he stretched, picked up the spade and, escorted by Romeo, went back to the wooden cart in the lane. Backpack slung over one shoulder, Callie trailed behind, watching as he stroked Foumi's flank and chucked the spade into the cart where it settled between a rake and a sickle.

"Actually, Michel," she began, rather shyly, "I've been rethinking my work and trying to do what you told me."

"And?"

93

"I'm very grateful for your advice. Thank you."

"You're very welcome." He began hitching the horse to the cart. "Sometimes all we need is an outside view that pushes us in the right direction. I know that I make a point of listening to what people tell me. They aren't always right, but their suggestions can't be written off without some thought."

"Although some people do like to force their opinions on you, and are determined to show you that their way is the right one. Then they push you, very subtly, to do things their way."

He leaned against the cart, one arm slung casually over its edge. "I think you're referring to the discussions you've heard at the retreat."

Glancing down, she toed the ground. Hesitated. Then raising her head, she met his watchful eyes. "Yes, I am. But that doesn't matter because I can't make out half of what people are saying. What I do know is that many of the artists there are working in a way that doesn't touch me."

"I can imagine that."

"I suppose you can. I think what is important," she continued, "is what you suggested I do—reduce, eliminate, narrow things down. I should start working with darker papers, too, see where that will take me. There's only one problem: I have no idea where to find pastel paper. Is there an art supply store anywhere in the area?"

"There is, but it's some distance away, in the town of Erblon."

"How can I get there? Is there a bus? Some other transportation?"

His sun-honed skin crinkled with overt amusement.

"You can always take Foumi and the cart."

"Okay, okay," she chided dismissively. "Go ahead. Make fun of me because I was kind enough to give you a compliment, tell you that I appreciate what you said."

He chortled. "You're the one who doesn't approve of my special blue van…"

"I didn't mean to offend you, honestly. I open my mouth and say the wrong things far too often. It's a terrible habit of mine." But she saw he was grinning and not at all upset.

"In that case, you're forgiven, and we can drive there in my precious, almost priceless, antique."

"Do you mean that?" She felt as though someone had just handed her a lovely and unexpected present. "Oh, thank you. But I can't go tomorrow because we're going to visit the artist Elise Grondin's studio."

"Good. I think you'll enjoy meeting Elise. So why not the day after tomorrow?"

"That would be super."

"Okay, I'll swing by and pick you up at ten thirty in the morning."

"It's a date."

"That, it certainly is." The warmth in his eyes almost took her breath away. Then she pulled herself up short. She had to cut this out. As nice as Michel was, as well as they seemed to understand each other, he was solely a friend—and she'd better make sure it stayed that way. A gardener—or an estate manager—might be a fitting erotic mate in a classic book like *Lady Chatterley's Lover*, but it would get her nowhere in the art world. "Thank you, again."

"My pleasure." His tone was easy and amused. "Didn't I mention that I'm always a sucker for a damsel in distress?"

She stood there, not moving, as, slowly, man, horse, dog, and cart headed down the lane and into the verdant distance. Strange. She didn't at all feel like returning to Froideval although evening was coming on. How much more pleasant it would be to stay out here, smelling the sweetness of weeds and seeing the sky turn dusky pink. *And where are these weirdly bucolic thoughts coming from, city slicker?*

Chapter Nine

In the morning, as she and the other artists waited
for Colette and Laurent to arrive with their cars, she
caught sight of Michel. He was ambling between the
stone buildings far beyond the vegetable garden, and
she couldn't help admiring his very solid, confident,
and masculine way of moving. How on earth could she
ever have thought him unattractive? *He looks
dangerous, enticing. Like a dashing swashbuckler.* As
he vanished from view, Callie slipped off the low wall
where she'd been sitting, determined to cross the yard
and find him.

Suddenly, here he was again, holding one end of
what seemed to be a long wooden beam. At the other
end was the captivating, wild-haired young woman she
had seen tending to the vegetable plot. Laughing, they
stopped, propped the beam against a wall, and stroked it
as if it were an animal, a horse like Foumi, or a canine
Romeo. Then Michel reached out, pulled the young
beauty into his arms for a hug—an overly affectionate
hug, as far as Callie could tell—and that stunning
woman full-heartedly participated in the embrace.

From her vantage point under the shadow of the
overhanging roof, Callie glowered at the two of them.
Why…that woman was a good twenty or thirty years
younger than Michel. *And so what*? Why was she
feeling jealous? There was no time to continue her

spying. The cars pulled up in front of them, and they all piled in, began heading down the long lane under the trees, through the dull village of Épineux-le-Rainsouin, and onto the main road.

Callie pushed disappointment to the back of her mind. Why shouldn't Michel have scads of women in his life? Hadn't Azeline warned her that he was a lady-killer? Yes, she had. And what she had to concentrate on now was the artist they were about to visit and not fret about romantic estate gardeners and their exquisite, broken-finger-nailed vegetable-planting lovers.

She was pleased to be part of this expedition for, knowing Elise Grondin's work, she was very much looking forward to seeing that artist's studio. However, she knew it would be nothing like the ones she'd seen in old photography books.

In those nineteenth-century Parisian ateliers, there had been high, soaring ceilings, paneled windows, and framed paintings had covered every inch of wall space. There were always musical instruments somewhere in the room, perhaps a cello or a violin, and often a piano. Dapper clients lounged on sofas, discoursing with smocked artists, and in each photo, a fleshy, sheet-draped model waited patiently.

Studios weren't anything like that anymore, Callie knew, especially not those belonging to artists who worked in the country. But as they pulled up in front of a narrow stone cottage in the middle of a small village, she was certain she wouldn't be disappointed.

The building, no doubt a poor peasant's abode in some earlier time, had been adapted for Elise Grondin's large works. Instead of a second floor, there was only a narrow mezzanine where papers, wooden chassis, and boards all tumbled from vertical shelves, and the entire downstairs workspace was illuminated by a high, north-facing skylight. Higgledy-piggledy, and spread over a multitude of long tables, were paint-encrusted plates, bottles containing indefinable mixtures, and round glass beakers filled with brightly colored earth.

The artist, a gray-haired woman with a disarming smile, was laughingly apologetic. "I've been working here for almost sixty years, and chaos seems to have taken over."

Chaos didn't bother her, for she created her tactile works in an unmethodical manner, randomly mixing powdered pigments with sand, grasses, rags, glues, or any pliable matter.

"I never buy conventional tubes of paint or other standard artist's preparations, and I never paint with a brush, so you won't find such things in my studio. Half the fun I have is experimenting, seeing what will work, what can be sublime."

She held out her hands, and Callie saw that the skin had been rubbed shiny, that her fingernails, clipped short, were deeply stained with color. "I want to confront matter, create different universes with matter."

On all the walls were examples of the artist's imaginary worlds: underwater scenes, blurred seascapes, landscapes composed of sticks and tangled vegetation. And everywhere, there was sheer beauty.

****

That afternoon, it started raining again. After lunch, Callie headed for the studio in the carriage house, settled into the same nook by the window. Ignoring the others in the room, blocking out extraneous noise, she began drawing—tentative strokes.

99

Working from memory, she eliminated colorful petals but outlined their shadows, concentrated on the indefinite space between remembered stems and blades of grass.

She thought of Elise Grondin's hands, stained and work worn; she remembered the fertile, dark soil between Michel's long, strong fingers. And, insistently, she rubbed, added rough contours, then layered, hatched, and crosshatched, smudged, softened here, and sharpened there.

She worked intently, unaware of all that was around her, and it was only hours later that she leaned back and loosened the kinks in her neck. Examining what she'd produced, she felt that once-familiar old glow of satisfaction, and it was as strong as it had ever been. She didn't know where this new way of seeing things and working would take her, or whether this heady pleasure would stay with her, but she had learned something essential at Elise Grondin's studio. And from Michel Alexandre.

She'd been so intent on what she'd been doing, she hadn't heeded the little knot of people sitting in a circle across the room, and she hadn't paid any attention to their discussion. Nicholas was with them—of course, he was—for he'd never shun talk about art. What were they conferring about now?

Nicholas caught her eye. "Why don't you join us, Callie? We're discussing new technology and how it affects the way artists are producing new works."

"New technology? Artificial intelligence?"

"That's right."

Did she want to go over there, sit with them? Did the subject interest her? Not really. She understood AI could be a viable tool for some, but she doubted that it could conjure up the same ecstatic high this afternoon's hard labor had brought her. Still, sometimes she had to show she was a good sport. Standing, she put her sketchpad aside, crossed the room, pulled up a folding chair, and as always, fought to make sense of the discussion.

"AI isn't creative or imaginative, although the compiling of images from random sources can approximate the creative process."

"It's a sort of collective unconscious. We have to harness its power, use it as a collaborator while maintaining ultimate control."

On and on they went. Callie's attention wandered. She shifted on her hard seat, stifled yawns.

"Shouldn't we be considering the ethical questions?" dark-haired Veronique asked. "Art is spiritual, emotional, but the art created by AI is neither."

Callie didn't care about AI, about the ethical questions, or about the collective unconscious. She was almost sliding down onto the carriage house's cement floor with ennui. How tedious, these long palavers that took time away from what she considered essential: working, discovering, challenging herself.

Peering out of the studio's broad window, she saw it had finally stopped raining. The emerald green of dripping trees beckoned to her, and she stood, waved to Nicholas, to the others.

"You'll have to excuse me. After a while, French is too hard to follow." Then, crossing the room, she packed up her supplies. If she were going to engage in debate, she'd rather do it with someone whose ideas she valued.

****

Tramping between the buildings around the château, she passed the spot where she had seen Michel just this morning, but there wasn't a soul around. Nothing to do but head out into the countryside, hope he was out there somewhere, planting, cutting, trimming, and urging frail little green things to take root and flourish.

She followed the now-familiar lane until she reached the scoop of the valley, but there was no sign of Michel. Of Foumi either, *and horses always leave odorous piles wherever they pass*. Still, he had to be somewhere out here, didn't he? She wondered where he lived—in one of those gray stone farmhouses perched up there, on the high hills above? *Why didn't I ask?*

Then again, how many personal questions had she asked him? Few enough. What books—if any—did he read? What did he do in his spare time? Where had he gone in his life? His English was perfect—why? Where had he learned it? What sort of paintings did he create? What medium did he use? Did he ever show his art? They had only talked about her work, her frustrations! Why, she was almost as bad, as self-centered, as Nicholas. She was ashamed of herself.

She thought about what Azeline had said—that Michel was a lady-killer. Hadn't she seen proof of that when he'd hugged that wild-haired beauty? Proof of what? A hug was a hug. You could hug lots of people without it meaning anything other than pure affection.

Not only that, but she and Michel had met three times. All three meetings had taken place in isolated settings. Had he ever made an advance? Had he ever flirted? Made a lewd suggestion? No, never! *Perhaps he doesn't find me particularly alluring, or thinks that I'm not worth the effort. I'm no wild-haired young beauty, that's for sure.* Not pleasant thoughts. But did lady-killers only go after beauty? No, they didn't. They went after anyone who was available.

Why did any of this matter? Because she liked him. She liked listening to him, hearing his deep voice, seeing the laughter in his eyes. A man like Nicholas dazzled with his beauty, but only at first. The dazzle hadn't lasted long…not for her.

She passed the spot where she had last seen Michel disappear with Foumi and Romeo, saw that the path forked. How far from Froideval had she come? Four kilometers? Five? Which direction should she take? Left or right? Both trails were narrow, sunken into the ground, and hidden in the shadow of overhanging hedges. Both were inviting; both were intimidating. Why hadn't she thought of bringing a map? *And where would a map get me? It wouldn't tell me how to find Michel, would it?*

How silly she was. Had she honestly thought she could locate him in this broad, rolling expanse? Heavy clouds were moving in; it was late, and the light was waning. If she wandered farther, it might be difficult finding her way back to Froideval. *Go on. Stop being a coward.*

She took the left turning and, under the deep canopy of green, the sky disappeared altogether. In the semi-darkness, she inhaled the ambient richness of rotted leaves, black earth, stagnant puddles. Those were the odors so familiar to her as a child. They were the same ones she had rejected—blocked out—of her adult life. *Why let old prejudices dictate my present and my future?*

A little breeze filtered through the greenery, set spring's vibrant young leaves dancing while tiny, white butterflies, pollen-laden bees, and hovering syrphid flies flitted between dazzling blooms.

She forged on, only halting when ankle-deep pools of water and boot-sucking mud prohibited advance. Winded, her feet aching, she collapsed onto the mossy bank and listened to the burble of water, the rustling of small rodents, snakes, and beetles busy in their parallel world.

How did it feel being here, crouching in a dank lane that had been carved out by unknown humans hundreds—perhaps thousands—of years earlier? She closed her eyes. *It's utterly sublime. It's like nestling in the moist underside of fragrant shrubbery.*

She sat, waiting for nothing. Just being. Only when she heard the first raindrops spattering gently on the overhead leaves, did she stand, head back to Froideval.

Chapter Ten

Callie spied Michel's van parked right outside the massive main door. How pleased she was that she would be spending a few hours in his company. She did her best to quash her enthusiasm—*I'm only relieved because I get to escape the long, convoluted discussions about art*—but she wasn't at all successful.

She raced up to her room, grabbed her handbag and the windbreaker, just in case those threatening clouds meant a new deluge, and headed back down the broad marble stairway. Which was when she caught them.

Below, their backs to her, Azeline and Michel were standing outside the library. They hadn't heard her, didn't know she was there, but despite the dimness of the light, she couldn't miss the loving look on Azeline's face as, laughing, she gazed up at Michel.

So I was right. Her heart plunged toward the floor. *She's probably in love with him.* And that affectionate arm, slung so casually over Azeline's shoulder, implied reciprocal emotion. Well…maybe. Maybe it was only a sign of amiability. *Oh, sure. Dream on. And, anyway, what does this have to do with you? Nothing. So what if Michel Alexandre is the playboy heartthrob of every single local female, be they frizzy-haired beauties or gracious women like Azeline?*

She didn't know—or perhaps she didn't want to analyze her feelings—why she was so angry, but she was. *How silly*. Hadn't she, just a few days ago, told herself to cut short any attraction she felt toward Michel? Hadn't she decided they were only friends? So where was this inexcusable, seething jealousy coming from?

Backing up, she shrank into the shadows, waited as Azeline and Michel moved down the long corridor. She heard the groaning front door open and close; then, on tiptoe, she continued on down the stairway.

By the time she reached the entry, Azeline was nowhere to be seen. Michel, however, was waiting outside, one strong leg slung casually over the stone balustrade. Dammit. How good he looked, lady-killer that he was, in those washed-out jeans, and in that denim jacket that outlined his heavy bear-like shoulders. And the bleak light only highlighted his sun-burnished skin. (*When is it ever sunny enough in this part of the world to tan?*)

"Ready?"

"I hope you haven't been waiting long," she said, trying not to sound peevish, only impersonal. To pretend she hadn't been witness to that amorous scene of a few minutes earlier.

Then, despite herself, she found herself wondering if Michel had spent the night here with Azeline. But no, that was a silly thought. Would he leave his highly conspicuous blue van right in front of the door for everyone to see? Perhaps he would…if he and Azeline were engaged in a long-standing fiery affair. What did she know?

Michel cranked open the tinny-sounding van door, and she climbed onto the seat with its cracked plastic covering. *Highly prized antique, indeed. Pull the other one*. Then they began bumping and banging down the main drive, through the leafy forest, and onto the main road.

"Callie? Is that a nickname?" Michel asked.

She pushed crabby thoughts of other people's romances—successful or unsuccessful—to the back of her mind. "Yes."

He waited for her to elaborate.

Which she didn't feel like doing. Then, feeling silly, she capitulated. "Okay. Right. Promise you won't tell anyone, but my real name is Calliope." She squirmed, waiting for mockery. How she resented her long-gone but airy mother for thinking that such a ludicrous moniker would be the right one for a girl born in the twentieth century.

But Michel was neither amused nor scoffing. "Calliope?"

"That's it. And I hate it."

"Why would you hate a name like that? Calliope was the goddess of epic poetry."

Callie sniffed. "Poetic references aside, try to imagine the taunts and jeers of other kids when I was young. My mother must have known that would happen, so why did she subject me to it?"

He remained sagely silent for a minute, but she did have the impression he was fighting a smirk. "I can see that the name Calliope might have caused problems back then. But that was long ago."

She laughed shortly. "Great! Thanks for pointing to my age."

He also laughed. "I didn't mean it that way."

"I know you didn't," she soothed. "But enough about me and my hated moniker. Tell me, why do you speak such good English?"

"Because I spent three years at an English boarding school."

"You did? Where?"

"Eton."

Callie frankly gaped at him. "Eton?" That famous and hallowed institution dubbed "the chief nurse of England's statesmen"? That had schooled generations of the aristocracy? And after an elite education like that, he'd become a gardener? She couldn't say that, of course—even she could clench her teeth and order her mouth to stay shut when absolutely necessary. All the same, she couldn't help blurting out, "Eton? You're kidding! It costs a small fortune to attend that school."

"True," he agreed. "I suppose you could say that I snuck in through the back door. I was always a pretty decent student, and my godfather was a former Etonian. He was the one who pulled strings, arranged for me to be accepted and to receive a full scholarship."

That explained some—but not all—of it. She couldn't know if he would resent her prying, so she waited, hoping he'd continue, give her more information. But he didn't. He only drove on, as calmly and carefully as the first time, taking sleepy country back roads, making sure to slow down for birds, even for butterflies and bees. Once, to her utter amazement, he stopped, got out of the van, and with a long stick, urged a dozing viper off the road and out of harm's way.

By the time they reached Erblon, the sky had cleared somewhat, and the threat of rain had abated. Michel parked right outside the medium-sized town set on a broad but shallow river. "It's more fun walking into the center," he explained. "Erblon is pleasantly picturesque, as you'll see."

Which, with its narrow cobbled streets and remarkable fifteenth- and sixteenth-century buildings, it definitely was. Callie noted the arched stone doorways, the Italian Renaissance window decoration, and the horizontal *cordons*—bands of ornamentation similar to those on palaces in Rome and Florence. "The architecture is very grand for a sleepy backwater of this size."

"Sure, it's sleepy these days," said Michel. "But because of its river location, it was a prosperous trade center until the middle of the eighteenth century. After that, the river silted up and became too shallow for the heavily laden craft, and the town's importance waned."

On the wooden gable of one more ancient house, she found the lovingly carved head of a horse beside another figure, a man. "He might have been an important ecclesiast back in the fifteenth century. See his pointed hat?"

"At around the same time this charming sculpture was made, the black plague was reducing the population of Europe by almost half."

"Still...don't you wish you could step into the past for a few hours, or even minutes, just to see what life was like back then?"

Michel grimaced. "I'm not sure I would. Time travel might sound exciting in books, but life as it was wouldn't be tolerable to us now. We're very much people of the twentieth and twenty-first centuries, and estranged from the medieval mentality. We would barely understand how people of that time functioned."

"And they wouldn't accept our behavior and social

mores either," Callie admitted. "We'd be burned as witches, sorcerers, or infidels."

"Undoubtedly. Picture what this town was like. This nicely cobbled gutter running down the middle of the street is quaint today, but back then, it was clogged with foul matter and waste. And even where privies, cesspools, drainage pipes, and public latrines did exist, effluent often leaked into the drinking water."

"Imagine the stench."

"And the traffic jams. Loaded pack mules, wood and charcoal vendors blocked every passage. Even main roads were extremely difficult to navigate because of the huge business signs on long poles sticking out everywhere."

"Don't forget the noise," said Callie, pleased to be pooling her knowledge with his. "The incessant clatter of horses' hooves and wooden wagon wheels on the cobblestones, the terrified screams of animals being slaughtered in doorways, the perpetual howls of professional mourners, and the cacophony of public criers who rang bells, tooted horns, chanted dire warnings or announced deaths, births, and public executions."

Michel winked. "Still interested in time travel?"

Chuckling, Callie winked back. "Okay, I'll admit it. I'd rather read about those days than live them."

The art supply store he brought her to was small, but packed to the brim with paints, papers, canvas, brushes, and the myriad other accouterments dear to a creative person's heart. Michel was obviously a frequent customer, and he was greeted with much earnest enthusiasm. *I suppose that's the advantage of working and living in a sparsely populated area. You*

don't have to be famous or successful to get attention.
Everyone knows who you are. As he chatted with the
owner, she went to the back of the shop and selected
large sheets of rough paper in dark blue, brown, gray,
and black. Now it was up to her to see what she was
capable of doing.

It was close to noon when they stored the papers in
the car, and Michel suggested lunch in another offbeat
locale, the café-restaurant in a famous former hotel
called La Boule d'Or.

"Why is it famous?" she asked and tried not to feel
elated at the idea of spending more time in his
company. He was so easy to talk to and such fun.

"It's a local curiosity. You'll see why."

The hotel sat in the shadow of a large thirteenth-
century church, and the main dining room had a time-
aged beamed ceiling and an uneven floor of red quarry
tiles. But the unique feature of the establishment was
the artwork. Ten large paintings, cracked and dulled
with age, covered every wall, and they showed a way of
life long gone: old-fashioned boutiques, empty dirt
roads, a pristine countryside, and a reedy lake without
boats or surrounding cottages.

She and Michel were shown to a corner table and
handed menus. "Do you eat everything?" he asked.

"Vegetarian food, preferably."

"Would you like me to order?"

"Please do."

The waiter brought a carafe of chilled rosé wine,
and Michel filled their glasses.

"What can you tell me about the artist who did
these paintings?" Callie asked.

"It's an amusing story. His name was Ezined, and

he arrived in Erblon in early 1914. He lived in a gypsy wagon with his wife and five children, and he made his living by painting signs and decorating cafés. Shortly after completing these ten canvases, he vanished from local memory. The people who owned this café-restaurant claimed that Ezined had died in the trenches during WWI."

"That's not very amusing."

"No, it isn't. Except, one hundred years later, in 2014, a man showed up in the restaurant and said he was Ezined's grandson. That Ezined had not fought in the war, but had continued crisscrossing the country and working. To prove it, he had some fifty signed canvases done by his grandfather, and they had been painted in the 1920s and 1930s."

"So why did the previous owners insist he'd died in the trenches?"

"Because they didn't want to admit that the artist had been an itinerant Roma. By inventing a more glamorous story, that of an artist who had perished in the war, they upped the status of these works of art."

"And if it weren't for his grandson, Ezined would be unknown today."

"Does that matter? These paintings aren't fine works of art. They're crudely executed, and rather naïve. Their importance is that they exist right here, in this café-restaurant. They show what this area was like a hundred years ago, and they represent something that has almost ceased to exist: what we call a painted café. There used to be hundreds of these, but most have been torn down, or the paintings have been covered over, or ripped out."

"What a shame," said Callie. She watched as the

waiter placed the entrée, two deep dishes of mushrooms poached in herbs and wine, on the table. The tang of hot butter, olive oil, and rosemary tickled her nose. She lifted her spoon, tasted.

"Good?"

"It's delicious," she said as, hungrily, she took another spoonful. "Your story about Ezined reminds me of something I saw many years ago, when I was an art student. One day, I happened to visit a very old lady, Martha Palmer. She was an author who had written one book only, a history about the street she lived on. The book never did find a publisher—who knows why— maybe no one thought it would sell. Martha lent me a copy of the manuscript, and I was happy she did so; it was a fascinating, well-written story, and carefully researched. When I went to return it, she showed me another room in her tiny apartment. There, stacked against the walls were paintings—how many? Forty? More than that? They'd all been done by her husband, and they were exceptional, semi-abstract landscapes. He had died years before, and now nobody was interested in his work."

"When artists aren't famous, and if their art hasn't sold well during their lifetime, it usually isn't worth anything after their death," said Michel.

"So if paintings have no market value, they vanish?" she asked. "I never saw Martha Palmer again because she died shortly after my last visit. She had no children. There was no one to inherit those paintings or the manuscript, so everything—all that original work— probably ended up in the dump."

"Most likely. But that's been happening for centuries, you know. Incredibly little of all that has been created—great literature, first-rate symphonies, paintings, tapestries, sculpture, works in stained glass, and fabulous architecture—has come down to us."

"Therefore, success here and now is what counts. It pays bills, gives you recognition, the satisfaction of knowing your work has merit, and that people are willing to pay for it."

Michel's brow furrowed. "You think that financial success is the most important thing? What if you have to subscribe to the fashion of the day in order to achieve it?"

It was a good question, also an uncomfortable one. How could she admit to Michel that she'd come to France hoping to charm and impress Nicholas, convince him to smooth her entry into the art world he was part of? How superficial she'd sound to an idealist like Michel—a man who planted trees for a future he might never see, who believed in rewilding, in protecting creatures as small as miniature dormice and as huge as giant elephants.

"I do know that I don't want to live in a teensy, noisy, ugly apartment for the rest of my life," she said defiantly. "I want a real artist's studio. I want to show my work, to have some success. Maybe you don't care about such things, but I'm not like you."

In response, here was that Gallic shrug.

Why was she sounding so aggressive? Why did she need to defend her ambition? Her desire to succeed? There was no reason…except she wanted him to know exactly why she felt so strongly about pursuing a goal.

Callie slid forward in her seat. "I did mention that I had an itinerant childhood, right? Can you imagine what it's like to move from place to place for years?

How it feels when you grow up on the back seat of a car, or drift from one loopy commune to the next? About having no schooling to speak of—aside from memorizing a few magic spells, hearing bad poetry, and learning how to look suitably pitiful while your mother begs on street corners?"

"Unpleasant," Michel conceded. "But you did manage to escape. You work as a curator. And you became an artist."

An unsuccessful artist, and only an assistant curator. But a fluffy herbed omelet and a side dish of vegetables cooked with elderberry flowers were now on the table, and talk of old miseries seemed silly with such tasty food in front of her. Callie lifted her fork and indulged full-heartedly.

"Yes, I did manage to achieve all of that," she admitted after quite a few mouthfuls. "But that was because my grandmother appeared on the scene like some vengeful fairy godmother when I was fourteen. Her second husband was a very staid Englishman, and they both decided that enough was enough. They wrenched me out of my mother's clutches and whisked me off to suburban safety. I was sent to school, given tutors so I could catch up on what I'd missed, and made to work hard. After that, because they believed in me, they pushed me to go to art school."

"You were lucky. But you couldn't have accomplished anything without your own will power." He smiled. "And your talent."

Talent? He thought she was talented? Perhaps he did, or he wouldn't have taken an interest in what she was doing. It was a thrilling thought, but she pushed it to the back of her mind…for the moment.

"Growing up with nothing didn't give me a great sense of self-worth. Being at the bottom of the social scale, I saw how other children lived. I, too, wanted to live in a cozy house in winter. I wanted to wear the clothes they did, not the rags my mother cobbled together. So, once I was an adult, I needed to hitch myself to someone bright and glittery." She paused, took a sip of wine. Did she really have to talk about all this? She must be boring him silly.

"Continue," he prompted. He even seemed interested.

Callie put down her glass and plunged on. "My ex-husband, Malcolm, was a charmer, a fast talker, a glib tooter of original ideas, a verbal creator, and people loved him. He'd had a bit of early success as an artist when he was young, and he could charm rhinos out of mud baths. The problem was, charm aside, he was lazy. As the years went by, he talked of the brilliant paintings he would produce, but they never came to life. There were several co-operative art projects, ones he pushed me to support financially, but they never amounted to anything. The few Arts Council Grants Malcolm received were never quite adequate—I didn't know why, and I didn't question him because I preferred to function on blind faith."

"That happens in many relationships."

"I guess so." Why was she still so angry? Why let her former husband ruin an enjoyable meal?

Callie put her fork and knife down on the empty plate. "Yes, many women—and men—fall into the same trap. I didn't know about Malcolm's gambling debts, about his five indebted credit cards, or the bank loans he had taken out in my name after forging my signature. So you see? I never want to be in that position again. Poverty is something I want to avoid for the rest of my life. Perhaps you're happy living in a lonely, isolated wolf's den somewhere in the backwoods, but I wouldn't be."

She regretted the hasty words as soon as they were out of her mouth…as she usually did. It was a shame, because she would prefer to remain on Michel's good side. Perhaps, deep down inside, he envied successful artists like Nicolas Trier but would never admit it. What did she know? And what did it matter? Her goal was to charm Nicholas, wasn't it? Then she noticed the sparkle in Michel's eyes. Why was he so amused?

"Callie? Why not look at things another way? Martha Palmer's manuscript is gone, and her husband's paintings no longer exist. Perhaps the most important thing was the pleasure both of them had in creating during their lifetime. Martha's writing demanded much research and rewriting; her husband's canvases meant trips to the countryside, a love of working with color, and the satisfaction of producing something startling. What happened to their work after their demise is of no importance to them."

What response could she give to that? She knew he might be right. He had been right in setting her out on a truly creative journey—and no one else at the retreat had managed that. She would always be grateful to him, but their ideas, their lifestyles, and even their goals were so different.

Dessert arrived—an apple baked with quince jelly and steeped in delicate sauce. Conversation veered away from ambition and turned to Callie's museum work, to the tin-glazed earthenware, porcelain, and bone china she was most knowledgeable about. But she couldn't help wondering if her mercenary declarations had, in some way, destroyed Michel's good opinion of her. Did that matter? Yes, it did. Very much. Why? Did she know? Desperately, she tried to unravel her confused emotions.

Chapter Eleven

"Excuse us if we're speaking too quickly for you," said a bearded young man whose name she had already forgotten. "Because you speak French, it's easy for us to overlook the fact that you are a foreigner and that you can't always follow what we're saying."

"Sometimes I can say more than I understand," said Callie, truthfully. "And sometimes I understand more than I can say. It's fairly confusing, so please, don't worry about me. The muddle will clear up, eventually. I'm just not used to so much arguing around a dinner table. Is it always like this in France?"

Everyone cackled.

"Sometimes discussions are so heated, people leave the table in a fury."

She smiled. "Where I come from, everyone avoids giving an opinion in case they offend someone else. That's better for digestion, but less interesting to watch. This is more like a meal in the middle of the arena at the Roman Colosseum."

Dinner over, all trooped back to the winter garden. Callie lagged behind, unwilling to join them. What she truly wanted was to climb the broad stairway, sneak back to that extraordinary bedroom of hers, and curl up with a book. *Unsociable behavior: I've been living on my own for far too long.* She hesitated, standing there in the hallway and chewing her lip. *If I don't watch out,*

I'll turn into a real hermit.

"Callie?" She felt the faint pressure of a hand on her shoulder. She turned, saw Nicholas smiling down at her.

"Why not come back to my atelier for a nightcap?"

It took her several seconds to register what he'd said, it seemed so unlikely. "A nightcap? Yes, why not?"

There! She'd sounded normal, hadn't she? No gushing, no excess, no jumping up and down with joy. Yet Nicholas Trier had invited her, not one of the others, not the blonde Marie-Jeanne, not puffy-lipped Katell, or cat-eyed Pascale, not Sophie. Unless...all the others *had* been invited and were already waiting for Nicholas to arrive.

"You'd better get a sweater or a raincoat. It's starting to drizzle."

Of course, it is. Any other type of weather would be too much of a shock to the system. But when she came back down the stairs, Nicholas was still there, alone, and waiting for her. So she had been singled out for this meeting. She couldn't repress the feeling of triumph.

Hadn't she known this would happen? Hadn't she been right? He had noticed her lack of participation in the long discussions that the others held with such zeal. By ignoring Nicholas, by keeping herself removed from the tight clique surrounding him, she had excited his desire to conquer. *How these vain men need love from all and sundry.*

Passing under tall oaks and skirting puddles, they followed the graveled lane to the carriage house. Neither spoke, and Callie wondered how he would proceed. What would she say if he asked if she liked his work? What words could she find? But why fret about that? Why would he seek her approbation this evening?

They climbed the stairs to the studio at the top of the carriage house, and in the faint light of one corner lamp, she saw the atelier was empty. No, no one else was here.

"Make yourself at home."

Home? She sat down in a rough twill armchair while he opened a bottle of red wine and fetched two glasses from a low cupboard. He hadn't asked if she wanted wine—and after the glasses she had consumed at dinner, she didn't—but why refuse now? Perhaps a little more of the stuff would put her at ease…because she was oddly wary. Why? She wasn't sure.

Nicholas took the seat opposite hers and raised his glass for a toast. "Santé."

"Santé."

He looked around the room. "My studio here is unlike the one I have in Paris, but it isn't unpleasant."

Good. A neutral, although unexciting, topic of conversation, and one she could participate in with glib ease. "It's a far cry from the sordid places many artists were forced to work in, especially in the nineteenth century. One element lacking in most was water."

"True. And many artists had only one room in which to work, sleep, prepare their paints, receive their models, their students, and their clients."

"If they were lucky to have any clients at all," countered Callie. No way would she confide that her own scrubby London flat could be a close match for the one-room studio they were describing. Except she did have water. And a toilet. And heat. And a shower. *Luxury.*

"Of course, the art world isn't an easy one to navigate," Nicholas continued. "How many people appreciate the significant role art plays in society? How it reflects the values, aspirations, and emotions of our modern communities?"

Thankfully, he didn't seem to expect a response from her, and he went on to speak of technology and the challenge it posed. "We have to find the balance between our artistic vision and commercial demands."

Callie leaned back in her chair, sipped her wine. Where was he going with this? Why was it any different from when the others were present? She was being lectured to, and his tone was downright superior. He spoke of his own work, its place in society, his contact with professionals—the ones who counted. Her experience, feelings, and ideas were of no consequence. She was here in the role of listener, the person elected to hear the famous man's theories on this evening. He was so certain she would consider this a privilege.

Perhaps it was her fault...in a way. Assuredly, Nicholas had sensed how interested she had been when they'd met in London. He must have noticed how she'd been watching him since coming here. *What he doesn't know is that his words don't interest me. That he doesn't interest me, either.*

It was true. The admission jolted her, and she almost felt like laughing out loud. Instantly, she thought of Michel. What would he say if he were in this room now? She could imagine—could almost see—the humor in his eyes, and the disinterest. He would never come out with such self-important logorrhea, she was certain of it. But wasn't that normal? Michel didn't seek success, but her own success might depend on this man in front of her. How did she feel about that now? Was it still something she would pursue?

"You have become friends with Michel Alexandre?" The sudden, unexpected change of subject startled her. Had he noticed her inattention? Read her thoughts? She knew she was flushing and hoped, in the dim light, he hadn't noticed.

"Friends?" She stalled for time. What was this about? She had sensed aggression in his question, knew it hadn't been innocent. What answer could she give? Had Nicholas seen Michel's van outside Froideval? Had he seen her drive off with him? If so, why was this a problem?

Unless…if Michel were an employee here at Froideval, perhaps he shouldn't have taken the day off to drive her somewhere. How was she to know what was possible? What was acceptable?

She understood so little of what was going on, who everyone was, what their positions were. Since arriving here, she'd felt as though she were dog paddling in an unfamiliar, chilly sea, not knowing which direction to take, or where the shore might lie.

"I don't know Michel Alexandre well enough to say he is a friend," she began cautiously. "He's an acquaintance. We've met, purely by chance, out in the area where I've been drawing. He's very pleasant company, and we talk about art, about pastels, and about nature." Surely, that sounded neutral enough. And innocent. Those words couldn't get Michel into trouble, could they?

Expressionlessly, Nicholas leaned forward and refilled both their glasses—Callie hadn't even noticed she'd emptied hers, and he hadn't questioned whether she would want more.

"I don't want you to take this in the wrong way, Callie. You are intelligent, and a woman of experience, but I should warn you. I did see you drive off with Michel Alexandre the other day." Pausing, he appeared to be troubled.

"We went to Erblon for art supplies." *Okay. So now he knows. And? Come on. Out with it.* Silently, she waited. Why did she again feel like a guilty fifteen-year-old schoolgirl, one who had been called into the director's office because she'd committed a misdemeanor?

Nicholas met her stare evenly. "Michel Alexandre isn't what he makes himself out to be."

Where, in heaven's name, is this coming from? "Oh?" Setting her wineglass down on a side table, she asked drily, "What, in your opinion, does he make himself out to be?"

"He seems friendly, easy to get along with, but the one thing that interests him is seducing women. He plays at being the untamed, savage spirit who lives in a stone cottage—and some women find that challenging, even romantic."

Could Nicholas be right? She'd seen Michel holding that wild-haired young woman in his arms; she'd seen him with reasonable, dignified Azeline. But would Azeline be attracted to a Casanova? Could she be one of those practical women who craved an unfaithful lover with a reckless streak?

"I know that there are women who think they can domesticate such men," Callie admitted. But she would say no more. Michel wasn't sitting here with them; he couldn't defend himself. That made this a one-sided witch trial.

"Of course, they can't domesticate them," Nicholas scoffed. "Men like that—as soon as one conquest has been made, they're ready for the next." He watched her steadily. "No doubt you think I'm wrong in warning you. You are old enough to know what you want. I just thought you should know how things stand."

And give me time to put up barriers? Or make sure I keep away from Michel. She tossed her head. "I'm only here temporarily, so I don't think I have much to worry about."

"Michel Alexandre has been known to take advantage of the women who come to the artist's retreat. Two weeks later, the woman has gone back to where she came from. She is forgotten, and the coast is clear for a new, more local, conquest."

"I see."

"You can accept that, as director of the retreat, I feel responsible for those who participate. I don't like people being hurt." He lifted his glass and held it up to the lamplight, as if approving the wine's ruby beauty. "There's something else you might not have realized."

"Oh?" *Now what?* Callie felt like covering her ears. She didn't want to hear more malicious gossip.

Lowering the glass, he contemplated, in silence, the far corner of the room, as if struggling with his conscience.

Why is he being so theatrical? Why is it so important to discuss other people's amorous affairs? Everyone is an adult. From what I've gathered, musical bedrooms is a popular night sport here at the retreat.

"You are a curator in a well-known London museum," he began. Leaning back in his chair, he fixed her in his gaze. "You know as well as I do that, in your position, you collect hangers-on, ambitious artists. I also attract such people. Why? Because I know the people who count—the critics, the gallery owners, the investors. Therefore, people want to be part of my charmed circle, and they attach themselves to me."

"Ah." *So that's where this conversation is headed.* Callie waited for him to implicate himself totally.

Nicholas raised one hand in a gesture meant to indicate resignation, also caution. "Your job as curator might be behind Michel Alexandre's friendliness."

Michel take advantage of her? Did he seriously hope she would help him set out on a successful artistic career? Did that sound likely?

True, such things happened all the time—hadn't she hoped for the same from Nicholas? But the accusation didn't sit right with her. Michel had never alluded to his ambition or questioned her about her position at the Glassover. Even if he had, she could do nothing. She was on the lowest rung of the museum's ladder. She had no power to influence that institution's decision makers, or to promote any artist.

Nicholas stood, went to the window, surveyed the dark, drenched park, the dripping trees. "There are times when I want to forget the more sordid aspects of human nature."

He's being dramatic again. That studied pose, that solemn tone, this shadowy room...it's like something out of a bad French film from the 1960s. It was always the same. Head held back, chin raised, he assessed the world from some lofty height. Strange how the beauty that had first attracted her to Nicholas had lost its power.

He turned back to her. "Let's change the subject. After all, Michel Alexandre isn't the most fascinating topic of conversation."

What, Callie wondered, was there left to say? He had managed to do a very effective character slaughter on Michel, one that even a certified saint wouldn't survive. Without the slightest attempt at dissimulation, she turned her wrist and looked at her watch. She'd been here in the studio for long enough—those glasses of red wine had effectively quashed all notion of time—and she was exhausted. How draining this exchange had been. How unpleasant. She stood.

"I'll walk you back," said Nicholas.

It was raining steadily as they set out across the damp grass, water oozing under their feet with a squeezing-sucking sound. *Not very romantic.* And her pretty shoes were soaked through.

When the massive front door was finally in front of them, Nicholas stopped. Slipped one finger under her chin. "You interest me, Callie." His tone was easy, and seductive. "I very much enjoyed our conversation this evening." Bending, he kissed her, just at the corner of her mouth. A gentle, affectionate kiss, not demanding, not aggressive. Then, turning, he went back over the grass and into the dense shadow of the trees.

Callie stood there, motionless, staring after him. Things were going the way she'd wanted, so why didn't she feel in the least bit triumphant?

Chapter Twelve

La nuit porte conseil, thought Callie—the French expression for "let's sleep on it." And early morning light did bring some clarity into the picture. As she dressed, she thought about last night's kiss. It hadn't been thrilling. Or sensual. Her heart hadn't thumped wildly; her knees had felt very strong, not at all weak and rubbery the way they should have when being kissed by a man she had desired for many months.

Nicholas hadn't kissed her out of any burning need. The kiss itself…what word would best describe it? *Unwarranted*. For if she had been a willing dupe in her younger years, she had since replaced naïveté with a good dose of mistrust. She knew nothing was as simple as it seemed.

Nicholas had said he'd enjoyed their conversation. Had it been a conversation? She'd hardly uttered a word, had merely listened. Was that why he thought her interesting? Good listeners always found favor with narcissists.

Then she pushed cynical thoughts out of her mind. Seeing her connection with Nicholas in anything but a positive light wouldn't fit in with her plan. Did she have a plan? If so, would Nicholas fit into it in any way? She didn't think so, not any more.

After breakfast, she joined the others on the front steps, for today, Nicholas had arranged for them to travel to the museum in Erblon, view that collection of nineteenth-century etchings that were normally kept from the public eye because of their fragility. She was uneasy at seeing Nicholas. Would he single her out for special attention? She hoped not.

She needn't have fretted. She was, again, no more than another member of the group. Katell and Pascale had taken up their rival positions as his favorites, and clustered together were the other admiring groupies. It was all so familiar, and Callie knew why, too. *He's like a cult leader.* Thanks to her mother, she'd seen a plethora of those. *I'd never allow myself to be trapped in their aura.*

In Erblon, they spent an hour in the museum's archives admiring the painstakingly etched lines that portrayed serene seascapes, a lone boat on the misty river, and huts hidden in deep vegetation—unique images of the past and executed with remarkable skill. Viewing concluded, they began climbing the stairs to the exit. Without warning, here was Nicholas, by her side. "Why not travel back to Froideval in my car?"

Why single her out again? *There must be a reason.*

"We'll go for a coffee first."

The café he chose was not the same archaic place where she had gone with Michel. This interior, fashionable, more impersonal, simulated a British pub. Modern copies of old hunting scenes covered the walls, as did several framed Beatles posters. Pint jars hung on hooks, and brown wood paneling looked suspiciously like PVC plastic. *Not very convincing, as far as "Olde Worlde" décor goes.* Even the servers were snooty.

Nicholas led her to a corner booth with (fake) leather seats and ordered coffee for them both. She folded her hands, waited for him to reveal why they were here together. But, once more, Nicholas talked about himself, the inspiration for his work, his philosophy.

"For me, the hierarchical difference between an object and any representation of that object can consist of the physical object itself or its depiction in various forms."

Although he spoke in English, she was too incurious to pay much attention. How thrilled she would have been, only a week ago, to be sitting here, alone with Nicholas. To be getting his take on the contemporary art scene. Would she have soaked up his words even then? Probably not. She and Nicholas operated at two different ends of the art spectrum, and those ends would never mesh. It was up to her to cut through the art-speak and obtain practical information.

She leaned forward. "Tell me, Nicholas, everyone talks about the galleries in Paris, about how lively the art scene is, but listening to the other artists here, it seems a very closed shop. Is that true?"

He observed her for a full minute, perhaps secretly annoyed at the change of subject. "Very," he conceded.

"And how did you do it?"

His little smile was smug, for he was proud of himself and his achievement. "Being an expert at communication helps. You need to master the strategies necessary in presenting your work correctly to galleries and wooing critics and bureaucrats. Being part of the newest trends in the art world is of the utmost importance. That is what I have been trying to tell you since you've been at the retreat, Callie." It was a reproach, no mistaking.

So here she was, forced to question her own ambition...again. Was she the sort of artist who adopted trends in order to be successful? Who followed a leader? No, she wasn't. If that meant that she would never be an artist of importance, that she would never earn money from her art, that she would continue to only show her work in restaurants, or in small group shows, or in very minor galleries, that was okay. Michel had been right: the importance was in creating now, at this very moment. *And doing it my way.*

****

Patrolled by the orbs of those grouchy elders in their golden frames, Callie was making her way down Froideval's long hallway when a small tour group oozed out of the formal dining room. She stopped, listened to the guide who pointed to the portraits and named the most renowned of the long-gone nobles: Albis de Razengues, Amaudric du Chaffaut, Aubert de Petit Thouars, and Julienne-Hippolyte-Joséphine, Duchess of Rienne. All had been people of power and importance, secretaries to kings, court figures, or powdered, rouged, and influential consorts. But now, Callie mused, outside of being wall decoration and fodder for tour guides, their deeds were forgotten.

"In 1789, at the dawn of the French Revolution, there were 120,000 aristocrats out of a population of twenty-six million," said the guide. "Today, although they are no longer the dominant social group and some grand names have become extinct, their number has remained constant or has increased. Why? Because they maintain a higher birth rate than other social classes."

As subtly as possible, Callie wedged herself between two stragglers as they were shepherded into the library, another palatial room of parquet floors and marble fireplaces, where walls were covered in frescoes "in the Italian style." And, up on the mezzanine, stored in Regency-era cupboards, some two thousand books were embossed with the arms of the Marquis de Bénou.

A visit to the Great Gallery was next. Here were portraits of women draped in luxurious cloths alongside harrowing hunting scenes with mortally wounded stags. On one far wall, an exceedingly large still life portrayed a dead pheasant, a bloodied rabbit, and a cornucopia of fruits. *It's all a bit too robust and gory for my taste.*

As they filed into the music room with its walls of pale blue, where Saunier desks and seating arrangements circled a harp and gracefully painted harpsichord, Callie noticed the guide was observing her with overt suspicion.

"*Vous faites partie de ce groupe?*" The tone was harsh and accusatory. No, she wasn't part of the group; she was a freeloader. Clumping together, the others turned and leered at her with know-it-all disapproval.

Red-faced, Callie backed out of the room and strode down the hall as purposefully as possible. How embarrassing! From their decorative frames, the haughty dead monitored her escape, and they were as chastising as the living.

She was about to turn left and go up the staircase to her room when, looking through one of the narrow windows near the entrance, she caught sight of a figure perched on the stone balustrade. *Michel.* She was amazed at how happy she felt at the thought of seeing him—*playboy that he is.* Grinning, she raced to the door and pulled it open.

Then stopped. She'd been mistaken. Basking in the

welcome rays of sunshine, the very distinguished Louis sat in exactly the same place where Michel had been only a few days ago.

Louis eyed her with some astonishment—of course he would. She smothered her wide-open grin, fought desperately to find a reason for its existence.

"I've just been chastised for gate-crashing a tour group," she said, as if that explained everything. "I attached myself to them thinking nobody would notice. But the guide did, and she wasn't very pleasant about it. Everyone gawked at me as if I'd committed some horrific crime. I can't tell you how silly I felt." She knew she was babbling.

Louis nodded sympathetically. "I know how you feel. I've also done some unsuccessful freeloading in my time."

Callie had to giggle. It was hard to imagine someone as dignified as this silver-haired man high-tailing it out of a room full of sneering rubberneckers. "It has certainly cured my nosiness—for this afternoon, at least."

"Not permanently, I hope. Azeline would be more than happy to show you around if you're interested in seeing all the nooks and crannies."

"I know she would," Callie admitted. "I should have taken her up on her offer instead of being sneaky."

"And did you like what you saw today?"

"Everything is so grand, and so elaborate. Perhaps too elaborate. I honestly think I might have been more comfortable living in a peasant's hut back then," although that declaration sounded fatuous to her own ears. "At least a hut is small and manageable."

"You think so?" Louis harrumphed. "A peasant's

hut? I doubt that. You wouldn't be able to cope with the misery. The poorest laborers lived in shacks without chimneys, with only a hole in the roof to let out smoke. There were no windows because few could afford to pay the window tax that lasted from 1798 until 1926. And because the huts were so smoky, doors had to be kept open, even in the middle of winter. That doesn't sound like a pleasant existence to me."

"How about something a little more upmarket?"

"There were disadvantages in the better places, too. Even in the early twentieth century, many peasant houses were nothing more than four rough walls with a roof and a chimney. Everything took place in one room—sleeping, eating, cooking, dying, mating, giving birth, mending, weaving, spinning, making and repairing tools. And living only a waist-high plank wall away, the family's cows, horses, and pigs provided warmth. Daily life must have been rather pungent."

"Very pungent. But some homes must have been nice and comfortable."

"That's a modern way of thinking," Louis said. "Yes, the bourgeoisie lived decently, but in the peasant world, comfort was shunned as a sign of self-indulgence. A house that was no more than a hovel discouraged the landlord from raising the rent, and the tax collector from demanding higher taxes. It also prevented neighbors from becoming jealous."

"Okay, I give up. I've been imagining Hollywood-style peasant cottages, and those never existed." She smiled at Louis, her curiosity piqued. "How do you know all of this?"

"Because, until my recent retirement, I was a history professor."

"You were? I had no idea." As usual. She'd always thought he was...well...a member of staff...maybe a sort of butler-server. *Got that wrong.*

Louis nodded sagely. "However, running a place like Froideval is even harder than a full-time teaching job: it's more like an obsession. That's why, years ago, Michel went to live out in that isolated stone house of his. I can't say I blame him. He needs solitude for the work he does. If he stayed here, in the main building with the rest of us, he'd feel hemmed in."

Callie scratched her head. This conversation had taken a very odd turn. As usual, she wasn't sure she'd understood anything at all. What—who—was Louis talking about? "Michel? Are you referring to Michel Alexandre?"

"I am," said Louis. "Only one Michel grew up in Froideval, as far as I know."

"Michel? He grew up here? In this château?" Even she heard her high, slightly hysterical squeak.

Louis studied her. Then he must have realized her confusion was sincere. "Of course, he did. He and Azeline are brother and sister. Didn't you know?"

Might as well be clear about her ignorance, even if Louis concluded she was an all-out idiot. "No, I didn't know," she admitted rather shamefacedly. "I think I've been walking around in a mist ever since I came to France."

"Don't worry," soothed Louis. "It happens to the best of us. Drop me in the middle of the English countryside, and I'd perish."

"Me, too," she mumbled.

"Therefore," said Louis, his expression sweet and kindly, "since nobody bothered telling you anything, you didn't know that Froideval was purchased by Michel and Azeline's grandparents back in 1920."

"No. I didn't know that either." She felt like crawling into a hole in the ground. Michel had lived in the midst of all this luxury and beauty? She thought about what she had told him, about the life she had led with her mother, about begging on the street. How embarrassed she was now. How humiliated. "They must have been very wealthy."

Louis guffawed. "Not at all. After WWI, huge estates like this one were being dissolved and sold for very little money, since maintaining them was too costly. Most were in an appallingly bad state after decades—even centuries—of neglect. Froideval was a ruin, and it stayed that way for seventy years. Even though the Alexandre family wanted to own a grand estate, and they had enough money to purchase this one, there wasn't anything left over for upkeep."

"So they all lived in a wreck?"

"Precisely. You should hear Azeline and Michel talk about their childhood, about freezing because, aside from burning the sticks of wood they gathered in the forest, there was no way to heat the rooms, and no money for fuel of any other kind. About the missing windowpanes they stuffed with old rags to keep out the cold. When the water was turned on, tadpoles flowed out of the taps, and birds nested in all the rooms. And in winter, banks of snow covered the floors, the furniture, even the beds."

"It sounds awful," she managed to say. *All that complaining I did. Why didn't he say anything, tell me about any of this?*

"Despite all that, Azeline and Michel were

determined to save the place and after Azeline and I married, so was I."

"You're Azeline's husband?" Things were getting stranger and stranger.

"Very much so." He chuckled.

"Oh. And how did you all manage to get Froideval into the excellent shape it's now in?"

"Years of elbow grease. We plastered, sanded, rebuilt, repainted. We had the roof fixed, windows repaired, and doors replaced. To finance everything, we began paving the way for green, ecologically oriented businesses to take over the crumbling barns, stables, and all the former estate farmhouses, and that happy solution did save this place. Now there are some twenty companies in residence. At the same time, the integrity of the old architecture has been preserved. Why? Because the people who are working here understand and respect what we're doing."

"Why would anyone—you, Azeline, and Michel—take on a project of such magnitude?"

"Passion," he said serenely, as if that were the only logical answer. "And because it's a way of preserving heritage, history, and roots. When you spend your life restoring correctly, there are incredible rewards. Once, years ago, we uncovered a fourteenth-century fresco of a lion. It had been hidden under layers of plaster, and it must once have decorated an interior wall of the destroyed stronghold castle. You find something like that, something that hasn't been seen for hundreds and hundreds of years, and your heart stops." He stopped, his face shining with remembered bliss. "Believe me, when we realized what we were seeing, the three of us sat there with tears rolling down our cheeks."

Reaching out, Callie fondly squeezed his arm. She could imagine how satisfying such an unearthing would be. "And the three of you restored this whole château on your own?" It sounded so unlikely.

"We started out on our own, but things have changed over the years. We receive government heritage grants that pay for artisans, and quite a few enthusiastic volunteers pitched in during the summer months. Of course the restoration isn't anywhere near finalized. The whole west wing hasn't been touched yet, and Michel is doing his best to bring the misused countryside back to health."

Louis stood, reached into his pocket, and pulled out a key ring. "You'll have to excuse me. Right now, I'm expected to drive into town for supplies or there will be no dinner tonight." He winked. "Azeline looks like a mild lady, but if I don't pull my weight around here, she'll have my head on a plate." And, saluting merrily, he left her there, sitting on the stairs.

Head on a plate? The English expression sounded cute—even funny—when spoken with Louis' strong French accent, but humor had temporarily deserted Callie. Her stomach clenched, and her thoughts reeled. She didn't know if she was more furious with herself, or with Michel. Why hadn't he said anything? Why had he let her believe he was nothing more than the gardener? Was he amused by her errors? Had he been laughing at her the whole time? What a rotten, lousy cad! Then, a new thought struck her, and anger receded.

Is the misunderstanding his fault or mine? Did I ever ask him outright what his job is? No, I didn't. Right in the beginning, I decided he was an estate manager or a gardener. Did I ask Azeline what her role was? No, I didn't do that either.

When she'd seen Azeline and Michel standing together, all she'd felt was jealousy. It had never dawned on her that they were siblings, or even cousins, or best friends. *How stupid.* Even worse, she realized what an uncomfortable position she was in.

Would Michel think she was interested in him because he owned—partly owned—a superb château, especially after her tirade about hating poverty? Did it matter if he did? Very much…because she *was* interested in him. But not because of Froideval.

Okay, then…so how does he see me? He's always friendly, and kindly, and he took the time to give me advice about my work, and he drove me to Erblon. But has he ever shown the slightest romantic interest in me? No. Never. And that was the most depressing thought.

Still, she had to set things straight, let him know she wasn't as mercenary or ambitious as she'd let him believe, as *she* had believed she was. Because, come down to it, she'd been fooling herself, lying to herself. She had to speak to Michel, tell him that. But how would she find him?

She wouldn't head out, comb the countryside, poke her nose into every hedge, swamp, or copse, because she knew how hopeless an enterprise that was: *looking for one particular needle in a haystack of needles.* She'd just have to wait for him to appear.

Chapter Thirteen

"Louis mentioned that you'd like me to give you a guided tour of the house," said Azeline. Then she smirked wickedly. "Unless you'd rather try sneaking into a tour group again."

Although squirming with embarrassment, Callie managed an indignant sniff. "How mean of him to rat me out."

"We're not very good at keeping secrets here."

Which Callie doubted. There seemed to be a whole conspiracy of secrets swirling around in this place. "If you don't mind, Azeline, I'd rather go see the west wing—the part that hasn't been restored—for a more exotic, less luxurious view of Froideval."

"Really? Then come with me now, if you have time."

"I certainly do."

"I hope you won't be too shocked by the state it's in. Even though most of the building looks good, nothing's been done to the west wing. There's enough daylight, so we can avoid falling into a yawning fissure and disappearing forever."

"It's that bad?"

Azeline winked. "No. I'm just trying to spook you. Michel always did that to me when we were children. Unfortunately, though, there are some dangerous places where the flooring does mimic swiss cheese. Michel and I used to play in the worst spots without our parents knowing—they'd never have allowed it. We liked imagining that the ghosts of guillotined aristocrats seeped up through the gaping holes and sought vengeance. Believe me, most of the time we scared ourselves silly. Michel was a brilliant storyteller, and he kept me fascinated for hours. Creeping around in scary places was far more thrilling than going to school."

He still is an outstanding storyteller, Callie thought. But so is Azeline. And like Azeline, she, too, was under Michel's spell, not that she would dare admit that to his sister—or to Michel, or to anyone else. But how she'd loved hearing him talk about history, about the countryside. His words had made France come alive for her, take form.

"Were many local people guillotined during the Revolution?"

"I suppose so, since there were portable guillotines set up all over the country. Historians estimate that some 15,000 to 17,000 people lost their lives that way. But another 20,000 men and women were shot, stabbed, or drowned during the Terror, and not all of them were dukes, marquises, or parliamentarians. Isn't it odd that movies, novels, and even history books encourage people to believe that it was only the moneyed, exploitive nobles and the powerful clergy who were murdered? In fact, most of the victims were commoners—carters, day laborers, servants—or war profiteers, political rivals, and country priests who refused to take the oath of loyalty to the Revolution."

"It must have been a terrible time. Why do you think it happened?"

Azeline grimaced. "Paranoia, I'd say. Rumors

141

about conspiracies and political infighting resulted in laws that enabled the execution of thousands of people suspected of counter-revolutionary beliefs."

They went into the library, and Azeline fetched a large key from a drawer. "There used to be an entry to the west wing at the end of the main hall, but it's been blocked up for at least a hundred years. We'll open it one day, if that part is ever renovated. For now, though, we only have access through the yard."

They passed by the servants' refectory, took the back door, and turned left at the raised beds of the kitchen garden where stalwart young green plants were poking up through the black earth.

"I love eating vegetables," said Callie, "but I'd never be able to identify them in a garden."

"Gardening isn't my overriding passion either," Azeline admitted. She stopped walking and pointed. "However, I do think the fringy things over there are carrots, and those are baby cabbages in the far patch. There are also some twenty different kinds of salad that Catherine always plants. She's a strict vegan, and positively fanatical."

Callie struggled to get her brain in correct functioning order. "I give up. Who is Catherine?"

"My daughter. She and Lucas, the assistant gardener, do all the work."

Callie thought about the woman she'd seen Michel hugging, the one who had conjured up such feelings of jealousy. "Is Catherine the beauty with wild red hair?"

"Beauty? Yes, she is." Azeline smiled proudly. "You can't miss her. Louis and I can't work out where that Celtic strain comes from."

Callie felt even more foolish. Catherine was

Michel's niece? How had she managed to get things so wrong? *Lacking in basic language skills, kiddo. Thinking that I'm making sense of everything, when all I've been doing is catching bits and pieces, then adding in some nonsense, and inventing the rest.* The only people she could understand correctly were Azeline, Michel, and Louis because either they spoke slowly or they used English.

So did Nicholas, she remembered, but that remote man wasn't the sort of person you could sit down with for a cozy natter. His discussions were stiff with cant. *Even when he's warning me that Michel is a Casanova, or trying to convince me that I interest him.*

They passed between a stand of plane trees, and here was the door to the west wing where the high windows were lacking glass. Others, she could now see, had been boarded up. And over all, were twisting, conquering vines. The place definitely seemed spooky. Callie was elated.

The studded wooden door wailed even more plaintively than the complaining main one they used every day, and Callie found herself in an entryway where shattered plaster obscured another majestic marble floor. Picking her way over the debris, Azeline led the way to a twisting wooden staircase, and each step was layered with dead leaves and discarded pigeon feathers.

On the first-floor landing, iron hangings suggested missing chandeliers, and high oak wainscoting bulged with damp.

"You see those fissures in the wood? When we were little, Michel told me that mysterious creatures called Haws lived behind the panels, and that sometimes their scrawny hands would reach out from between the cracks, snatch people, and drag them into their loathsome netherworld. He even had me put my ear to the wall, and believe me, I could hear those awful creatures moving around. I was terrified."

"How mean of him to do that to you!"

"You think so?" Azeline's tinkling laughter filled the dusty space. "I loved it, loved being scared out of my wits. I delighted in thinking there was an alternative, invisible world close to ours, even if it was a mysterious, frightening one. Michel was three years older than me. Because he was a boy and very sure of himself, I was confident that he'd rescue me if a ghastly Haw hand ever tried to claw me away."

They followed a dim passage, empty except for one rotted chair, where the powdery, motionless air was heavy with defeat. In one room, strips of fine tapestry dangled, and just before a graceful, red marble fireplace, an impressive but ripped meridian joined four carved chairs in a conversational group.

"It's almost as if the furniture is waiting for guests that will never come back."

"Oh, Michel assured me they did return. He swore he'd seen them, and I believed him implicitly because he described everything in grisly detail. He claimed that, just before their arrival, a misty cloud filled the room along with an eerie chill that could frighten the stoutest soul to death."

"Nonetheless, you were both brave enough to come here, play in this part of the house?"

"Of course. Michel said we were safe because we only came in during the day. Even he would never risk being inside this ruined wing after dark. At night, he would come to my bedroom, sit on my bed and tell me other nightmarish ghost stories. I believed in all the phantoms he invented—especially in the waif."

"What waif?" Callie loved ghost stories.

"He claimed that she was an orphan who had been locked out of the house by her cruel nanny in the seventeenth century. The little girl had died of cold, but her ghost still came here on winter nights, scratching on the windows, and begging to be let in. He said if I ever saw her, I wasn't to open the door or I'd be carried away and frozen into a snow-girl."

"And did she appear?"

"Of course she didn't. She only existed in Michel's imagination—and mine. Just like the terrible ghosts who lived in one of the back bedrooms. Come, I'll show you, although I'll admit I feel edgy each time I go in there."

In the shadowy corridor, darkened rectangles on the faded wallpaper evoked long-vanished paintings. "Art that went to pay my grandparents' and parents' debts," Azeline explained as she pushed open a door.

The room was much like the others in this unworldly palace of rot and blight. Here, too, were high ceilings and shattered plaster, and the shredded curtains were a memory of the precious brocade they had once been. A high-backed wooden bed was half collapsed, and a snowstorm of feathers cascaded from its tattered mattress. Along one wall was a hulking armoire.

"Its doors are locked, and we never had the nerve to peek inside. Michel claimed this bedroom had been abandoned long ago because whoever slept here heard atrocious screams and terrible moaning. That, in 1823, when the owner of the château called in the gendarmes to investigate, they discovered a heap of skeletons immured in the floor."

Callie noted that the fairly solid oak flooring was untouched. "So he made that up, too?"

"Of course, he did. And after Michel went back to his own bed at night, I'd lie in mine, convinced that all manner of evil things lurked under the mattress, and in every shadow. I sometimes felt menacing tentacles reaching for my ankles or heard rasping creatures as they slipped under the sheets. The only way I could escape the ghouls was by falling asleep."

Callie's eyes widened. "You managed to sleep? Telling you those tales was a terrible thing to do to a little girl."

"Don't you believe it, Callie. Michel's bedroom was right next to mine. I knew he'd come running and protect me if I called out. And with his prodigious, wild imagination, he made my life far more interesting."

"Or shockingly picturesque."

"Luckily," Azeline insisted. "We never had a television, and unlike other schoolchildren, we never did normal things like going to the movies. All our entertainment came from Michel's stories and the books we read, all sorts of books—fairy tales, history books, novels, and scientific books. There are so many books here in Froideval, and they made up our social life. They had to. We lived so far from everywhere, and we had no friends to play with. Our parents discouraged all visitors—especially children from the village—from coming here, because they didn't want outsiders to see the terrible state of things, or know how impoverished we were. They preferred to have everyone think we were living in luxury in an enchanting castle."

"But the other part of the house, the east wing—it wasn't as ruined as this part, was it?"

"Not so disastrously ruined, but not that much different. The roof leaked badly, and rain cascaded into the upstairs rooms each time there was a storm. The electricity was dicey; we only had hot water if we heated it up on the stove in the kitchen, and even as children, we washed our clothes by hand. I don't think any of us owned a pair of shoes without holes."

"And your parents didn't mind living like that?" What Azeline was describing sounded so much like her own childhood—minus the stately home.

"Our parents didn't pay much attention to us. Despite having no money, they flitted about the countryside in elegant secondhand clothes—social butterflies living on illusion and other people's dinner parties. Michel and I were supposed to entertain ourselves, fix our own meals, be independent." She hooted. "You should have seen our culinary efforts. We had a sandwich competition that lasted for far too long because we tried to outdo each other in creating something original with poor supplies. The worst I made was a water sandwich. Imagine two soaked pieces of bread—it tasted awful—but I had to eat it, roll my eyes in ecstasy, and claim it was delicious."

Callie had to laugh, despite the sadness of the tale. Yet Azeline didn't seem in the least troubled by her past. She hadn't let it ruin her present happiness. "Your family life sounds similar to my own. Of course, trying to be comfortable in a ruined manor sounds more attractive than living in a car in a public parking lot, or in a farmer's field, or sleeping on the floor in the apartment of yet another of my mother's short-term boyfriends."

"That was your childhood?" Azeline asked. "I'd never have pictured it that way. You seem so self-confident, so tidy. Your hair is always perfect, you're so neatly dressed, and so in control of your emotions."

"That's how I appear?" *Of course I do. Stiff, and prim, and trying too hard to look acceptable.* "Isn't it funny? All my apparent control comes from being confused much of the time. I understand you because we're alone, there aren't any noisy debates going on all around us, and your descriptions make everything so interesting." But there was no way Callie would admit how wrong she'd been about everything. That she'd thought Azeline was Michel's sweetheart. That would be going too far.

Azeline smiled wistfully. "Nonetheless, Michel has always been more creative in his thinking than I am. I still wish he'd come, sit by my bedside at night, and tell me ghost stories. He has such a knack for making life so rich. We all presumed he'd become a writer one day, but as we know, he uses his creativity in many ways."

Callie repressed a deep sigh. Yes, she understood perfectly. *Imagine falling asleep beside Michel, feeling his warmth, and hearing his terrible ghostly stories in my ear. What delicious fun that would be! Dream on...*

Chapter Fourteen

The next morning, as she passed down the corridor, Callie noticed that the door to the library was open. As nosy as usual (despite the occasional humiliating setback) she couldn't stop herself from tiptoeing over and peeking in. *I never do learn my lesson.*

There, leaning over a table and examining the large sheet of paper spread across its surface, was Michel. He didn't see her, and she studied him from the doorway. With that burnished skin, strong, aquiline nose, high brow and receding hairline, he was incredibly sexy. *He makes every other man look insignificant.* Why had it taken her so long to accept it?

Had he sensed her presence? He looked up. When he saw her, his intense, dark eyes bored into her. Was that tenderness or just interest? Or something else altogether? Whatever it was, it didn't seem like he was annoyed with her, or with the silly mercenary things she'd said.

"Hi." It was all she could come up with. Why was she suddenly so shy?

"Hi yourself," he returned with one of those slow, lazy smiles that always made her heart flip.

She stepped into the room and crossed over to the table. "Why aren't you at work planting trees?"

Michel pointed to one long window. "See what's going on out there? We call it a blue sky with sun.

Planting season is over until the fall."

"I see." So that was why he, Foumi, and Romeo hadn't emerged from behind a jaggy hedge or been highlighted on a hill's top edge when she'd searched for them. *They aren't a fixed presence in the countryside, silly goose.*

She took a deep, rather shaky breath. "You never told me you grew up here in Froideval. That it belongs to you and Azeline."

"And Louis," he added. He wasn't in the least bit disconcerted.

"Okay, okay." Feeling edgy and very much betrayed, she tried not to succumb to his charm. "But you let me think you were the gardener."

"But I *am* the gardener." His eyes had begun twinkling. He evidently had no regrets about having led her on.

"Don't be fatuous," she puffed with annoyance. Then realized what he said was indisputably true. *He's the owner, and the gardener, and the restorer, all of those things.* Still, he didn't have to look so amused by her silly mistake, did he?

Slowly, the humorous sparkle dimmed. He must have realized she was being serious.

"Callie?" he began quietly. "I didn't tell you that Froideval belongs to me, and Azeline, and Louis, because I thought you knew. Everyone else does."

"Well, good for everyone else," she said crossly. "*I* didn't know, and no one mentioned anything to me."

"Since that's the case, it was an oversight, not a dark secret. Anyway, you could have found the information on Froideval's Internet site. Our names are there, for everyone to see."

"Oh." Callie's mind raced. Hadn't she searched for details about Froideval on the Internet? Yes, she had, but she'd only wanted to see photos...of the château, sure...but mainly of Nicholas Trier.

"And by the way," Michel continued, "I'm also the landscaper, and one of the wildlife conservationists. Being part owner of Froideval means that I can carry out those duties without worrying that the land will change hands and, once again, be victim to destructive practices. Happily, Catherine and Julian have been raised with the same ideas, and they're as determined as we are."

"Yes, I know who Catherine is. *Now* I do, because that was finally explained to me by Azeline. But Julian? Who is he?"

"Azeline and Louis' son."

"Oh." Who else was going to show up? "Your nephew?"

"Right. Julian isn't here because he's in Rouen, working. Normally, Catherine would be with him."

"She would?"

"Of course. When Catherine isn't digging around in her vegetable patch, she's a carpenter, and very determined to use artisanal techniques. She often goes with Julian as a consultant, only, at the moment, she's working on a restoration project in Erblon. "

"And Julian does what?"

"He's an architect, a very radical one. He's constantly fighting colleagues who refuse to integrate the old and traditional into their work, who erase the past and justify themselves with false intellectual arguments. Too many think they're superior to the artisans of another epoch who used simpler tools and natural materials. But how can we ignore the negative impact of concrete and plastics that can't be recycled?"

At a loss for words—how many other things had she misunderstood?—she glanced down at the table, at the large sheet of paper he had been bending over when she'd entered. It was a map, one crisscrossed with lines and swirls.

"An Ordnance Survey map?"

"Right. I love maps like these, and I can pour over them for hours. The best show all the hills, valleys, and lanes that once crossed this area, the paths that led from farm to farm, village to village, and that were in constant use. Traders took them, and tinkers, pilgrims, peddlers, even brigands. Sadly, many are gone because farmers have plowed them over, but walker's associations are fighting to preserve those that remain."

"I took one sunken lane the other day," Callie said. Of course, she wouldn't admit she was looking for him. "I walked past the place where you were replanting and found myself deep below the hedges and trees. It was…magnificent." She could see how pleased he was. Why did it matter to him that she was beginning to appreciate his world?

"I agree," he said with extraordinary tenderness. "Magnificent is the right word for it. I often go there. Did you know that you were walking in the footsteps of local tribes who lived in this area in pre-Roman times?"

"It's that old?"

"Beyond doubt. And they used those same sunken lanes in their struggles against the Roman invaders."

"They weren't very good at it," she retorted. "Gaul was conquered, and it became just another part of the Roman Empire."

"Ultimately, yes. But those canny Celtic fighters did put a strain on the enemy. Just imagine the rows of Roman legions, all decked out with their unwieldy shields, cudgels, weapon belts, arm guards, plumed helmets, and segmented armor. Only a short distance away—maybe as close as an arm's length—were the Celts with their long hair, mustaches, and naked, tattooed bodies. And hidden by the thick greenery, hunkering down in the sunken lanes, they spied on the army's maneuvers. Then, with guerilla tactics and sheer agility, they inflicted the most debilitating casualties."

Callie giggled. "You see? You're doing it again."

Michel cocked a questioning eyebrow. "Doing what?"

"Telling stories. Azeline told me you were an extraordinary storyteller, that you had a fervid imagination, and that everyone was convinced you'd become a writer, one day."

He threw back his head with a roaring, bellyaching peal of laughter, and Callie couldn't help chuckling along with him.

"A writer?" he gasped when he finally caught his breath. "My devoted sister exaggerates my abilities."

"How so? She says that you kept her terrified for most of her childhood, conjuring up guillotined phantoms, rattling piles of skeletons, and ghostly girls who tapped on windowpanes."

He was grinning proudly, but he shook his head in denial. "Come, I'll show you where all my literary prowess comes from." He led her up the small staircase to the mezzanine, where the high glass cases contained those precious, leather-bound tomes. With a sweep of his arm, he designated the many hundreds of volumes.

"Do you see these titles? *The Dictionary of the Sacred and Profane*, *The Catalogue of Judges and Consuls of Merchant Paris, 1526*, or *The Illustrious Poet, Alloys de Guevara*. Who reads such books today? Who ever read them? Probably no one. Maybe they were only collected for show, and for status. But down here, things are different."

Kneeling, he opened a low wooden cabinet. "These are what did interest people. These books are the ones people read for pleasure." He held up a volume with a worn cotton cover and well-thumbed pages. "Look at this: *Blossier's Collection of the Supernatural*."

Callie crouched down beside him and peered into the cabinet. Some of the books were in English: *Thrilling Victorian Ghost Stories*, *The Collected Works of Edgar Allen Poe*.

Michel pulled out other volumes, those stacked, pell-mell on the bottom shelf. "All are filled with ghastly, ghostly tales. And here," he said triumphantly, "is where I got my inspiration. Those ghouls, spooks, and revenants I conjured up for Azeline came from these pages. All I did was situate them here in Froideval." His chuckle was self-deprecating. "So what do you think of my imagination now?"

"I'm still impressed," Callie said stoutly. "You told the stories in such a way that they *sounded* believable. I bet you even added gory details, ones that you invented, just to make sure that they were frightening enough."

"Guilty as charged. You know what? Half the time I was as scared as Azeline. I believed what I invented."

"I understand perfectly," said Callie, her mouth tugging into a smile. "I had no older brother to tell me stories, so my secret world was filled with dryads who lived in oak trees, and naiads who resided in ponds and rivers. I'd lean over every bridge, spying on the trolls who lived there, and I knew, without any shadow of a doubt, that the plaster gnomes in people's gardens came to life when no one was looking. I met frog princes, saw fairies dance the night away, and I was ever on the lookout for fearful witches who would carry me off if I strayed too far."

"You see how lucky we both were?" said Michel with evident satisfaction. "We grew up without television. We didn't become passive watchers. You, me, Azeline, we all developed our secret worlds."

"And we all became artists in our own way."

"I can't imagine a life without creating art," he said, his face oddly serious.

"Either can I."

Sitting cross-legged on the floor, almost—but not quite—touching, she wondered if he knew how often his eyes laughed. She was captivated by his fervor as he talked about the colors that inspired him, the shapes he produced in his paintings. *Perhaps one day he'll even show me his work. And what if I don't like it? So what! It's the determination that counts, the love of expressing yourself.*

The sun slipped past the library's heavy curtains, played across the dark wood, made ornate molding shimmer, and held them in a gentle circle of gilded light. How long did they sit there, chatting about fantastically disparate subjects? Callie couldn't remember when she had enjoyed a conversation more. *And this is the man with whom I should be on my guard—according to Nicolas.* But, as always, Michel's behavior was that of a good friend, and not a cad.

They were both chortling at Michel's story of being chased across three fields by an amorous sheep, when the sublime moment came to an abrupt end. Azeline poked her head around the library door.

"There you are, Michel. We were looking all over for you." With her was a woman Callie had never seen before. Tall, ravishing, with shining red-gold hair tumbling over her shoulders, her mouth was full, her legs endless, and her startling violet eyes turned up prettily at the corners.

"Michel," she crooned in a racy contralto. "We had no idea where you were." Ignoring Callie, she came up to the landing where they had been sitting.

Michel got to his feet. "Hello, Garance." He kissed her on both cheeks.

Okay, thought Callie sourly, he didn't kiss her on the mouth, but it was close enough. Like it or not, there had been something intimate about the gesture, an impression confirmed when that woman linked her arm through his in a familiar, highly proprietary way. *And by the way she's pretending I don't exist.*

"Garance, this is Callie, one of the artists here at the retreat," said Azeline, who would never forget her manners.

But Garance still didn't glance her way. She merely addressed Michel. "Now that we've found you, isn't it time we got going?"

"You're right," said Michel. Turning to Callie, he hesitated. Was that pure regret she saw? One microsecond later, the look was gone. She must have been mistaken. With a little wave, the trio headed back down the little stairway and out of the room.

Callie followed behind, her feet dragging and her

heart heavy. All the magic had evaporated. She tried cheering herself up: *I'm just a temporary figure in Froideval.* Only a few days more, and she would be leaving, heading for the streets and cafés of Paris, and then returning to London. She might not even see Michel again while she was here, especially if he were tied up with that uppity Garance, whoever she happened to be. *And people had better not try to convince me she's another sister, or cousin, or grandmother, or niece, or wicked stepmother. Phooey.*

Why fret? There were other things to look forward to. Tomorrow, all the artists would be traveling to MAX's studio; the day after that, there was the big opening at the museum in Grenache. *So you see? What difference does it make if Michel has a hundred million beauties falling at his feet?*

But it *did* make a difference! It made a difference to her. Why? Because she would have given anything to have more of Michel's company. To hear him, to laugh with him. To share dreams and ideas. And then what? *Because Michel has his life here, and it has nothing to do with my own.*

She thought of Azeline, Louis, Catherine, and Julian, their passion for meticulous restoration. Of Michel, with his love of growing things, books, and painting. How much she had learned by coming here; her life would never be the same again. *Silly girl. Half in love with the most unavailable man on the horizon.*

Chapter Fifteen

"Callie? There's something I'd like to show you."

"Now?" Callie asked. "But we're going to see MAX's studio, and we'll all be meeting outside in about ten minutes."

"You have enough time," Nicholas said with that same little smile that, once more, didn't quite reach his eyes, or transform *his* skin into humorous wrinkles. *Does he ever laugh out loud? Is there a cheery side to this man? One that I haven't discovered?*

Nervously, she peered out of the long window— this was an excursion she didn't want to miss—but aside from two artists sitting on the steps and chatting casually, no one else was out there.

What was so urgent? Not wishing to offend and always polite (*it'll end up being my doom, this eternal politeness*), she followed Nicholas to the back of the house, out into the courtyard, past the vegetable garden, and into the old carriage house.

"Let's go upstairs to my studio."

Nicholas pulled up a chair for her in front of a large screen. "Now, take a look."

Obediently, Callie sat and watched the black-and-white images flicker. What was there to see? Upside-down people, then a narrow hallway, another person— man or woman?—blurred, undefined, striding back and forth.

She turned to Nicholas. "What are you trying to show me?"

"The energy behind it."

"What energy?" Resentful at being called away, at being forced to appreciate what she couldn't, she resisted.

"Its rebelliousness. Experimental video breaks the mold of traditional photography—either portraiture, landscape, or film—and extends its boundaries."

There's nothing new or original in what he's saying. He and the others have been through this a thousand times in all the long discussions. Why was it so important to bring me here at this moment? The work she was trying to do, the art she appreciated—neither had anything to do with this video, or with his theories. Surely, seeing the work of MAX in his atelier was more essential.

She took in the bleakness of this "personal" space. There wasn't a speck of dust, not a paper was out of place, and no filled waste bin poked out from under a desk. Who tidied up after him? Hardly the clinging vines, Katell and Pascale.

"Video is not only an important part of contemporary art history," Nicholas was saying, "but it reinvents itself through technological innovations."

So what? Get to the point. She'd been here for far too long. Surreptitiously, Callie peeped at her watch.

Did he notice? Certainly. And sensing her impatience, her desire to leave, he pulled up a chair, sat down beside her. "And I was wondering if you'd be interested in collaborating with me on such a project."

She gaped at Nicholas. "Me?"

He was smiling, that cold rictus.

Wasn't this precisely what she'd hoped for in coming to the retreat? She might have been thrilled if he'd made the same offer a week or two ago, but even then, the excitement of working with Nicholas wouldn't have lasted. He must know she would be of no help to him in this domain. Those who always surrounded him—his loyal fans—were far more competent, and willing.

So why was she here? *Unless he only wants to prevent me from going with the others, seeing MAX's work.* Why would Nicholas do something like that? Professional jealousy? Why even try to figure it out? The reason could be of no importance to her.

She stood. "Nicholas, I think we'd better discuss this another time. I have to join the others."

He also rose. "But when the others are around, we can't discuss anything of importance. There is too much noise. People are always trying to get my attention."

Yes, she was right. He was doing his best to hinder her departure. *How very odd.*

"I have to go before it's too late." She turned, was about to head for the door, when she felt his hand on her arm.

"Callie…" His voice was softer now, provocative. "Stay." Letting go of her arm, he reached out, cupped her chin. The prelude to another kiss? *Another unwarranted kiss.* Art-speak and the promise of working with the celebrated man weren't keeping her here with him. *So now he's trying seduction.*

Pulling away from the hand, she went to the door and quickly raced down the steps. Once outside, she rounded the stone outbuildings and half trotted to the front of the house. Stopped. There was no one around.

They had all left without her.

She felt like bursting into tears, howling. Turning this way and that, she hoped to catch a glimpse of someone's car, someone who had left later than the others. Then stood there, miserable. Furious, too. With Nicholas. With herself.

She heard someone coming along the gravel walk beside the house. She waited. Lugging a heavy blackened chunk of an old stump, Catherine appeared. There were corkscrews of wood shavings in her wild shock of hair, and a pale beige coating of sawdust extended from her eyebrows, over her eyelashes, and down to her heavy work boots. Resembling a substantially munched termite hill didn't seem to bother her in the least, and her "*bonjour*" was as cheery as ever.

"They've all left without me," Callie wailed, although she knew that Catherine would have no idea what she was talking about.

Catherine stopped in her tracks and studied her. "Who did?"

"All the other artists. We were supposed to go see MAX's studio together."

"So what?" said Catherine. Despite the massive chunk of wood she was carrying, she managed a Gallic shrug of her slender, saw-dusted shoulders. "Just go by yourself."

"How can I? I don't have a car, and I have no idea where it is."

Catherine's powdery brows shot upward. "Why do you need a car? Just walk down this drive that's right in front of you, and when you see the first path in the middle of the forest, turn left and go straight. It's not

161

even a kilometer away."

"It isn't?" Callie croaked, as weakly confused as she usually was.

"Of course not. Why would he want to live farther?" With that, Catherine and the wedge moved in the direction of the stone huts behind the house.

Why would he? What an odd thing to say…or was it? Wasn't this just one other thing she hadn't understood? Thinking too hard for speedy movement, she began inching her way down the driveway and entering the canopy of trees. Far too belatedly, outright suspicion had woven itself into knowledge. And dread. She'd done it again. Been wrong. How idiotic she felt.

Here was the path Catherine had mentioned, leading arrow straight through the forest. No one on earth, not even she, could miss the trace of wagon wheels, of horseshoes in the friable ground. She felt like slugging herself; she felt like collapsing, right under that big leafy tree, covering herself with the heap of last autumn's leaves and staying there forever.

Why was she so stupid? Why hadn't she worked it out before this? Why hadn't she asked Michel more questions? Why hadn't she even wondered if MAX meant Michel Alexandre? Why?

She knew the answers, all right. Because she'd always underestimated Michel and his talent, despite what he'd taught her, despite what Azeline had said about his creativity.

And why had she gotten things so wrong? Because Madame Besnard, a chiding, cackling woman who owned a café, had told her that Michel painted poor, horrible, blue things with two red eyes on one side of their head. The crazy thing was, MAX—a.k.a Michel—

really *did* paint gruesome things with rosy orbs, and he did it brilliantly. Because he was an *outstanding* artist, no other word would do.

In front of her, the trees thinned, and in a small clearing, she could just make out a long, low structure in rough granite. It was a traditional cottage, one that snuggled deeply into the hillside and was topped by a vegetal roof alive with twisting vines and bright wildflowers.

Tentatively, she came closer. On the far side of the house, a long, much higher extension blended equally into the slope. It was made of old windows, row after row of windows, each one topping another, then going higher still. Windows of every variety, age, and size fitted together like pieces in an abstract picture puzzle, until reaching yet another luxuriant green roof. Beyond question, that was his studio. How inspiring it must be to work in such a place.

She could hear people talking inside—the group from Froideval. Did she have the courage to join them? To face Michel? Feet dragging over the damp, muddy yard, she approached a wooden front door that was slightly ajar.

Why feel so ashamed? Did Michel know she had underestimated him? Desperately, she tried to remember if she had said anything deprecating in all their conversations, but she drew a blank. She could be forgiven for not knowing he was MAX, couldn't she? His artist's name had never come up when they were together.

She pushed open the door, stepped inside, and found herself in a main room with a floor of time-worn red quarry tiles and more walls of rough stone. On the right, there was a vast fireplace, and just overhead, wooden beams glowed with an oily ruddiness. And, everywhere, there were MAX's brilliant large paintings. On them were people, their faces distorted in joy or sorrow. Some fought, others groveled or pushed. Masses clumped together; twisted streets formed a hellish labyrinth; yet it was the brilliance of his bold strokes, his wild use of color that injected power into utter chaos.

The voices were coming from another part of the house, and stepping through a low doorway, she found herself in the bright space of windows. Yes, this was the way an artist's studio should be. Canvases were propped against the walls, here below, and up on high shelves. There were several easels; there were spattered tables with half-squeezed tubes of paint; there were old smeared rags, and jars of paintbrushes, knives, paint scrapers, and spatulas. From the walls, a thousand images assaulted her, and the heady scents of turpentine, of linseed oil filled her lungs.

In one corner, shelves were stacked high with art books; beside them, a sagging sofa sent out its welcome. There were nooks, secret places, and what appeared to be almost irredeemable clutter, but Callie knew better. What was disorder—even anathema—to an outsider, was, to Michel (as to Elise Grondin), a necessity. Woe to anyone who attempted to tidy!

Of course, Nicholas had tried to prevent her from coming here. Of course, he had! He'd known she would be impressed. Because Michel's influence might be stronger than his? Because he was in charge of the artist's retreat, not Michel, and he wanted to keep the upper hand? How silly, and what a useless struggle.

Collaboration was what made life exciting, not rivalry.

As discreetly as possible, Callie moved over to the group standing around Michel as he explained his technique, his inspiration. He glanced in her direction, and briefly, their eyes tangled. Blushing, Callie looked down. When she dared raise her head, he had turned back to the others.

And, like the others, she listened. He wasn't pedantic when he talked about art—he never would be, she knew that, by now—and he wasn't arrogant. He spoke as a true storyteller, with anecdotes that made all laugh, and a warm-heartedness that would defrost any hard heart. No wonder she had fallen hook, line, and sinker for the man; what woman wouldn't?

And there, just behind him, dressed in fashionable togs and artfully arranged in a director's chair, was Garance. Unsmilingly, she appraised the visitors with what seemed very much like irritation. Of course it was. This crowd had interrupted the intimacy of the afternoon.

Turning her head, Garance noticed Callie, and the glare she sent her way was distinctly hostile. *Where did that come from? I'm only an innocent bystander, not a rival for Michel's attentions.* Although, yes, she had to admit it…she wished with all her heart that she were.

And, come to think of it, what was someone as open and giving as Michel doing with a snooty, venomous lady like that one? Well…perhaps he was a man fascinated by beauty. Why not? He was an artist. She had been similarly flawed once upon a time.

Soon enough, everyone in the group was thanking Michel for his hospitality. Then, they began moving off.

What she would have given to stay here in the bear's lair—but that was impossible. He had never invited her before; why would he invite her now? The lady of the moment was the comely Garance. So, along with the others, she trudged back through the woods to Froideval. And every step of the way, she felt like kicking herself.

Chapter Sixteen

The exhibition was being held in a large, new, two-story contemporary art museum in the port city of Grenache, some fifty kilometers distant. All the artists stuffed themselves into the cars that were available, for no one wanted to miss an event as important as this opening where Nicholas, along with other bright stars, was showing his work.

Callie had seen Nicholas leaving ten minutes earlier, clad in his spiffy tweed jacket, a yellow silk scarf wound around his neck, his golden hair gleaming. He had slid into a shiny red sports car driven by a short tough dyed blonde with a hard, very red mouth.

"Her name is Monique Mottet," Laurent informed her. "Supposedly, she's his power agent." Nicholas had only given the briefest nod to the clutch of artists gathered on the steps of Froideval. Clearly, this afternoon, he was taking seriously his role of star, and loyal fans were lowly hoi polloi. Even those entwining vines, Katell and Pascale, although done up to the sexy nines, weren't singled out for special notice. As Nicholas drove away without them, they wilted like yesterday's blooms.

Soon all were roaring down a busy highway. No question of fine scenery now, for Grenache was a commercial city of some importance. Designated as the city's showpiece, the museum was constructed in the ubiquitous steel and concrete of all new architecture, and its towering glass front shot up into the clouded sky, mirroring the dull heaven above.

"Just another horrific trap that murders the thousands of hapless birds that crash into it," Callie groused to no one in particular. "Why don't architects ever take that into consideration?"

In the lofty open space inside, slender men and women dressed in black were setting out bottles of champagne. On long tables, sat tiny glasses containing frothy concoctions in pink, orange, and green, and silver trays held miniature puffed pizzas, pastry squares with goat cheese and honey, smoked salmon, and skewers of herbed vegetables.

Threading her way through the crowd of fashionably weary men with five o'clock shadows and carefully styled, just-out-of-bed hairdos, the perfume-soaked women dangling jewelry and click-clacking in their needle-thin heels, Callie approached the exhibited works.

All were large; all were accompanied by explanatory texts. Rusted and dented corrugated iron was explained as "an arrangement that confronts the viewer with an industrial object, thereby reinterpreting communication." Large white bedsheets on which photos of nudes had been printed inside squares were "autonomous architectures that question the principles of intimacy." Further along, twisted, stuffed sausage-like material slid, snake-like, along the walls: "An object that, by its unique size and volume, questions the space it occupies." It was succeeded by a long line of closed umbrellas: "Installations with open forms and approximate contours that seem to occupy the available space."

In one darkened room, huge backlit screens showed the same pretty woman's face from different angles, interspersed with photos of a beach. On the opposite wall, the same woman in a pink dress lay on a grassy lawn. Callie read the accompanying text: "Without intervening on the existing architecture, the over-dimension of the installation challenges our perception." And here was Nicholas' work—large letters imprinted on fictional flags—and explained as "a study in current events without geographic limit."

"Well, all that should keep us on our cultural toes," Callie grumbled morosely. Now what? How long would they have to stay here? Despondent, she found an empty guardian's chair, sat down, watched people as they circulated, talked loudly, and posed. Admittedly, a few did peruse the art objects, and some even emitted little cries of excitement. But the thrill of observing others wore off fairly quickly.

Finally, to her great relief, there was a call for silence, and the crowd gathered around a man holding out a microphone.

The first to speak was the museum director who, in a long-winded, rambling way, blathered on about the building's beauty and the importance of the exhibition. Then it was the smug city mayor's turn, and a beet-red regional senator accompanied him. They, too, jawed on endlessly about the beauty of this building and the prestige of the exhibition. Then the microphone was handed to an over-enthusiastic and largely incomprehensible art critic who informed them that it was an honor to be in the presence of so many eloquent interpretations of our society...or something to that effect. It sounded very wordy and self-congratulatory.

As usual, Callie's French, although somewhat improved over the two weeks, was far from good enough to follow what she suspected was no more than officious twaddle.

At last, it was time for corks to pop. Gratefully, she sprang out of her chair, grabbed a glass, and sipped the chilly, bubbling champagne. Then, greedily, she proceeded to gobble up as many delectable hors d'oeuvres as possible. At least showing the work of prominent artists in a prestigious setting did mean that the snacks and drinks were top-notch, and that was the only positive way to see this adventure. But, once hunger and thirst were quelled, she had to admit she was fed up.

She longed to be back outside, taking to the lanes around Froideval, drawing the murky green spaces between flowering vetch, dog violets, cow parsley, and cowslips. It would be her last chance to do so—also the last chance to see Michel, just in case she happened to run into him. The day after tomorrow, she would be leaving this area for good.

Staring drearily out of the museum's unnecessarily voluminous glass front, she saw the wind catch leaves, scraps of paper, and debris, twist all into mini-tornados. A tin can bumped jerkily along the gutter. How far away was Froideval? Perhaps she could find a bus that would take her as far as the little village of Épineux-le-Rainsouin. She could easily walk to the château from there.

Feeling someone clutch her elbow, she turned. It was Monique Mottet, Nicholas' agent. Her shiny red smile was tight and ambitious, her heavy perfume overwhelming, almost nauseating.

"It would be beneficial, Callie, if we could have a talk together, perhaps discuss things over a little dinner somewhere."

"Of course," said Callie, thoroughly mystified (as usual). This woman wasn't interested in her own work, was she? Perhaps she was enlarging on what Nicholas had suggested the other day—collaborating on a project together—although that struck Callie as being extremely unlikely. It was also, she now knew, not in the least bit desirable. "What things would you like to discuss?"

"The exhibition for Nicholas at your museum."

"*My* museum?" Callie's jaw dropped. "You mean in London?" Had Tessa, unknown to her, been in touch with Nicholas? Had she decided that his work would fit into the Glassover, after all? If so, why hadn't Tessa contacted her? She knew where she was. She had her cell number.

"Yes, of course. His London exhibition at the Glassover. We want to work out all the fine points with you," Monique continued. "We have to fix a date, know how much space will be allotted, what resources are available. Then there are all the other, more down-to-earth details." Monique Mottet wrinkled her nose in what was an unsuccessful attempt to look cute. "You know. The more mercenary aspects."

"I'm sure you do need all that information," Callie answered. "But I'm hardly the person to give it to you. I don't program shows at the museum. I have no say in the matter."

"What do you mean?" Monique's face tightened.

"Has Tessa Sharp, the museum director, been in

touch with you?" Callie asked. "She hasn't told me she's planning an exhibition for Nicholas. You really must speak to her."

"Why should I? You were the one who told Nicholas that you were arranging for his work to be shown. That it was up to you."

"*I* did? Did Nicholas tell you that? Believe me, I never would have said such a thing. I'm only an assistant curator, not a museum director. I work in the museum's pottery section, not in contemporary art."

Monique's icy blue eyes narrowed. "If this is so, what you are telling me now, then you have come to the artist's retreat at Froideval on false pretenses. Nicholas made certain you were accepted because you told him you had influence at your museum. Nina Portifo at the Ripple Gallery told us that was why you were present at his show in London."

Callie pulled back her shoulders and stood straight. She wouldn't let herself be cowed by this aggressive woman with her gory, mean mouth. "Perhaps that was what Nicholas *thought* Nina said," she began slowly. "Or maybe Nina wanted Nicholas to think that she had important contacts. But it isn't true. And if I was only accepted at Froideval because Nicholas—and perhaps you—made a mistake, I don't mind. I've enjoyed my stay there very much. I can't begin to tell you how much I've learned."

"Don't think you will again profit from our good intentions," Monique Mottet snapped. "I'll make sure that any attempt you make to show your work falls flat, you can be sure of that. I dislike liars."

As if you have the power to do something like that. Boiling inwardly, Callie glared as the woman turned on her spiky heel and was swallowed up by the crowd. How unfair! The attack had been so unjustified.

What a crazy situation. Never had she misrepresented herself. On the contrary, she was the one who had thought of using Nicholas for her own ends. And, all the time, he had planned to use her. That was why he had made those vague, insincere attempts to charm her. Why he had wanted to keep her away from Michel, his artistic rival (or so he imagined). The whole situation was funny…in a way. Perhaps one day she'd be able to howl hysterically about it, but that was the last thing she could do right now.

What she did want was to escape. To leave this palace of bloated words, this sycophantic crowd. Pushing her way to the front door, she headed out into the street. Perhaps she could find the train station here in Grenache, get as close as possible to Froideval, and then telephone for someone to fetch her. Surely, Louis wouldn't mind doing that. Or would he? What if Monique had been right, that she had been accepted under false pretenses? Would that matter to Louis? To Azeline? To Michel? *Why would it?*

She headed toward what might be the center of this city she didn't know at all. The already pummeling wind had picked up, and cars whipped past her on the busy roadway. Industrial buildings followed more industrial buildings, and car parks, and blinking electronic advertising screens, and highway overpasses, and speedways. Where the hell was she? *If I have one sure talent, it's for getting myself into a mess.* If she saw another human being out here, she could ask for directions, but there wasn't a soul around, just cars, trucks, motorcycles, ambulances, and vans. On she trudged…got nowhere that looked like anywhere.

Resigned, she marched across a windswept concrete plaza, reached one of the huge glass and steel buildings, and pushed on the door. Which stayed resolutely shut. Of course, it would. Today was Saturday. These were office buildings. No one was around. Okay. She had to head back to the museum and wait for the others to take her back to Froideval.

She began retracing her steps…and realized she was hopelessly lost. Where was that glassy repository of horrors? Perhaps straight ahead? And why did everything have to look the same? Didn't city planners and engineers have any imagination? A left turn took her into a shabby high-rise housing estate where, from a rubbish-filled alcove, a clutch of youths in hoodies scowled with dead-eyed hostility. No, this was definitely wrong. Turning, bent forward to fight the gale, she retraced her steps. And felt the first hard spatters of rain. *Right! Just what I need.*

Spatters turned into a torrent of water. Her drenched hair, released from its pins, fell in a soggy curtain around her shoulders. The pretty sprigged dress she'd chosen to wear for the opening clutched her thighs and knees like super-strength cling film, and her shoes were long bathtubs that squished out waterfalls with every step. There wasn't even a bus shelter in which to hide, just this thundering road, and as each car passed, oceanic waves engulfed her. Miserable, she trudged on. Yet, she couldn't help but see the irony of the situation: *this is where I came in. What a country!*

She sensed, rather than saw, the dark blue car pulling up beside her. She ignored it—of course she did. What sort of pervert would stop for a drowned rat on an empty stretch of urban disaster? Only someone who meant trouble. She forged on ahead.

"Callie!"

She stopped. Turned, and attempted to identify the driver through the deluge.

The car door had swung open. "Get inside this car!"

"Michel?" How was this possible?

"Now!"

"Yes, yes, yes, yes, yes," she muttered. And did as she was told. Her wet clothes squealed dreadfully as she slid onto the seat, and instantly, a small lake formed around her.

"What are you doing here?" she managed to squeak.

He ignored her question. "Where the hell do you think you're going in a storm like this?" He sounded angry.

"It wasn't raining when I left the museum," she said, miffed. "I was only trying to find the train station so I could get back to Froideval." For some reason, it sounded incredibly silly.

"Don't you ever look up? Didn't you notice how dark the sky was? Haven't you heard the storm warnings?"

"What storm warnings?" she grumbled.

"On the radio, on the news, in the newspaper."

"No, I didn't. I don't read any French newspapers, and I don't listen to French radio." Why was everyone yelling at her today?

Michel only grunted, then reaching into the back seat, he grabbed a thick cardigan. "Here, put this around you until we can get you into some dry clothes. I'll turn up the heat." The car began splattering through the huge, rough seas of water. Then, once again, they were on the highway and heading out of the city.

"Where are we going?" She tried to stop her teeth from chattering.

"Home."

"Sounds good to me." *I'm soaked, bedraggled, ice cold, and I should be feeling utterly miserable. But I'm not.* Something more like calm—or was it pure bliss—engulfed her. She wasn't in that awful museum, she wasn't being berated by Nicholas' monstrous agent, and she wasn't lost in a concrete world. No, she was here, in this car, with Michel, the nicest, most wonderful man she had ever met.

From the corner of her eye, she peeked at him. Evidently, he was still annoyed. "It's sort of funny, don't you think? I mean, in a way, it is. Here you are, coming to the rescue of a damsel in distress yet again."

He shot her a look that contained only the faintest hint of amusement. "Obviously, you like making a habit of this."

"That wasn't at all my intention." She squeezed out the words between teeth that were clacking like castanets. "What are you doing in Grenache? You weren't at the museum? And this isn't even your car!"

"No. It's Azeline's car. And, by the way, I was in the museum with Garance, and I saw you on the other side of the room. Then, seconds later, you were gone. When the rain started, I came out and started searching for you. I had the feeling you'd get into trouble. You have a talent for it."

"Of course I do," she admitted sheepishly. "I do it so often, I get in a lot of practice."

He only harrumphed.

"But if you drive me back to Froideval, Garance will be stranded."

"I doubt that."

"I'll bet she'll be very cross. She's part of your fan club, isn't she?" Callie knew she was fishing for information.

That he didn't give her. "Getting you into dry clothes is more important than worrying about fans," he said, bear-gruff.

After that, there was nothing to do but concentrate on not shivering, letting Michel get on with driving through the blinding torrent, and basking in the pleasure of his company. Being rescued definitely had its good side—even though that good side could only be fleeting.

Chapter Seventeen

By the time they arrived, the wind was gone, and the rain had lightened to a mild, summery drizzle. After passing the gatehouse, Michel drove under the canopy of trees, then turned right and headed down the rough, unpaved lane, not straight on to the château.

"Why are we going to your place?" Callie asked, overawed by the thought of being in that wild, personal interior with its forceful paintings. "If you take me back to the main house, I can change, get out of these sopping clothes."

He didn't bother answering. Pulling the car alongside the stone building, he parked, then came around to her side, opened the door and grabbed her elbow like a vise. "Come on."

As she kicked off her soaked shoes at the door, Romeo rushed forward to greet them both with the usual canine excitement. He didn't in the least mind her drenched apparel. Michel disappeared through a low doorway off the main room and came back with a heteroclite pile of clothing in his hands.

"Put these on." He jabbed his finger at another door. "The bedroom's in there. The bathroom and shower are right next to it."

"You like ordering people around, don't you." But she didn't mind in the least. She examined what he'd handed her—a sweatshirt, large jogging pants, and thick wool socks. "These things are huge. I'll look like a chimpanzee in them."

Now the corners of his mouth did twitch. "A dry chimpanzee."

"True. But I'd prefer a little glamor instead of the decked-out circus animal look."

"Go," he ordered.

Her wet feet made flapping flipper sounds as she made her way to the bedroom. And what an impressive room it was, with a beamed ceiling and rough walls. One long window gave out onto a canopy of green, and she could hear birds chirping happily now that finer weather was back.

On the far side, there was a huge bed covered with a multicolored hand-woven spread. Callie tried not to think of all the beauties, the women like Garance, who had lain there. *His private life has nothing to do with me!*

She inspected the other items of furniture, and they were undoubtedly as old as those in the château, but far more rustic: a hand-hewn peasant table, two chairs with straw seats, a commode, and a large wardrobe, all unpretentious and pleasing to the eye. And on the wall, were more paintings, not his own, but delicate pieces, the works of other artists—hazy landscapes, delicately wrought clouds—the sort of pictures a man who loved gentleness would choose.

Gentle? Yes, it was true. He was gentle, and kind, and intelligently lovely. He'd cared for his sister when she was little and he was only a neglected young boy himself, and she knew he would care deeply for any woman he loved. Again, she thought of Garance, the hostile knockout, and her heart hardened. That wasn't the sort of person he needed! Then she pushed jealousy away. What claim did she have on Michel? None. What did her opinion matter?

Stripped down, showered, then dressed, she caught sight of herself in the mirror. In Michel's clothes, ones that were at least four sizes too large for her, she was at least dry. Also, very unattractive. Her usual L-shape had been transmogrified into a large, lumpy I. *Awful.* Without a comb, she couldn't be bothered pinning her hair into its usual twist, and it was too wet and straggly for styling anyway.

She waddled into the main room, saw that Michel had lit a fire. She watched him for a minute, noted the flames highlighting his strong profile. How strikingly handsome he is, she thought for the umpteenth time. *How incredibly seductive.* She settled into an armchair close to the fireplace, and he handed her a cup of something hot.

"What is it?"

"Grog, just to make sure you don't catch a cold. Rum with honey, lemon, and cinnamon. Drink up like a good girl."

She sipped. It was powerfully strong. "I'll be tipsy and dancing nude on the table top in seconds flat."

His eyes twinkling for the first time that afternoon, he made himself comfortable in the armchair opposite hers. Grunting happily, Romeo curled up between them.

"Tell me why it was so urgent that you leave the museum."

She remembered what Monique Mottet had said and felt dreadfully embarrassed. How could she tell Michel that she had come to the retreat on false pretenses? "Do I have to?"

"Yes," he said. "You do."

She stalled, took another sip of grog. Then capitulated. "Okay. To start with, I didn't want to be there, in that ugly building, anymore. Then there were all those pompous, awful speeches."

"They always are like that at openings of any kind."

"I know. I have to listen to the same sort of bloated rubbish at the Glassover, each time there's a new show."

"Go on."

"I don't know what you think, but I found the exhibition incredibly tedious. I mean, who wants to read pages and pages of documentation? Not me." She hesitated. Why not leave things there? Did she have to say more? She looked at Michel. Expressionlessly, he was waiting for her to continue.

Playing for time, she finished her drink, put her empty mug down on a little table beside the armchair, and curled her hands together. "Okay, here goes. After those speeches, and the drinks, and the food, things got mean. That awful bully of a woman—Monique Mottet, Nicholas' so-called agent—came over to me and told me that she and Nicholas wanted to know about the exhibition I had arranged for him at the Glassover Museum. And when I told her that I had no power to arrange any show, that I had never promised Nicholas anything, she said that I'd been accepted at the artist's retreat under false pretenses."

"She did?" Michel looked disgusted.

"She definitely did. She claimed that Nicholas had pulled strings for me to be here, all because of what I'd promised. And there I was, feeling like a fraud, even though I would never promise something like that."

"Then why feel like a fraud? Anyway, she was the one who was lying."

Mystified, Callie rubbed her forehead with the palm of one hand. "Lying about what?"

"Nicholas doesn't select which artists come to the retreat. It's a committee decision. There are eight of us who review the work of all the candidates. Nicholas has a say, naturally, but his is only one vote. I have a vote, a few members of the Arts Council have a vote, local artists like Elise Grondin, whose studio you visited, also votes, and we always diversify. No one trend or technique is favored since we work closely with the regional council and depend upon grants. If Nicholas did all the choosing, every artist there would be copying what he does."

"Then, why would Monique say that?"

"Perhaps she felt foiled. Or Nicholas did. They were convinced you'd be able to help them, and suddenly, there they were, confronted by their own illusions."

"How silly. All Nicholas had to do was ask me about my position at the Glassover."

The fire crackled. Any remaining humiliation evaporated into the toasty air. She felt snug and happy in this shadowy old room where generations of people had trudged through the centuries. Those bold, startling paintings no longer daunted her because they were a part of this man sitting across from her. They were his creations. They were fierce, and so was he.

"Are you hungry?"

She peered at him, stunned by the sudden, homey subject. "How can I be? I stuffed myself silly at the museum. I was so bored, I couldn't think of anything else to do."

Michel smiled...finally. That affable smile that folded into deep crinkles. Her heart beat a little faster. How she loved seeing the warmth that filled his eyes, that turned her heart into melted butter! She tried to quash her happiness, warn herself that any romantic feelings for Michel were uncalled for, and they would also be unwelcome.

"That was hours ago," he said. "Do you like tomato soup?"

"Who doesn't?" she said. Nothing like down-home domesticity to quash—or at least hide—gooey sentimentality.

"Good. My niece Catherine's greenhouse is filled with early tomatoes, and she was kind enough to share them with me. I think what you need now is a bowl of hot soup."

"You like to cook?" she asked shyly.

"I do. And you?"

"I'm not very good at it, probably because I've never tried to be. I only do stuff like salads..." She had to force herself to remain seated and not jump to her feet, bound around the room with joy. He was keeping her here, in his bear den, for dinner. Wasn't that nice.

He stood, looked down at her, smiling. "I like your hair like that. Loose." Reaching out, he touched the still-damp strands. Their eyes locked, and he waited, motionless. Somewhere in the room, a clock ticked, an old clock, deep and uneven, echoing the beating of her heart. Callie's skin tingled, aching for his caress.

Then he wasn't smiling anymore. Slowly, very slowly, he reached down, pulled her to her feet. Callie stopped breathing altogether as his fingers traced her chin, then moved to her ear, to her eyelids, then followed the shape of her lips. *Be careful*, screamed the shrill voice in the back of her head. *He's a professional seducer.* But that nasty little voice had no effect at all.

As if weighted, her lids closed when he lowered his mouth to hers in a tentative kiss, fleeting, and over far too soon. She gazed at him, waiting—hoping—for more. And, with a knowing leer, he kissed her again, this time with more need. At the brush of his tongue, the kiss deepened, became another thing altogether, something supremely wild and splendid.

Moaning softly, the blood sizzling in her veins, she slid her arms up around his neck, struggled to get closer, and he drew her, bulky, terrible clothing and all, into the hard, broad warmth of his embrace. One kiss led to another, sending waves of desire ricocheting from the tips of her ears, to the ends of her toes, and then back. Until, breathless, they pulled back, studied each other, and his eyes were heavy with something that almost looked like love.

"I guess what just happened proves that clothes don't make the woman," she quipped, but her voice was muted, husky.

His strong hands crept beneath the substantial sweatshirt and up along her smooth back, conjuring up a new trail of blazing sparks, before returning to encircle her waist. "Long and lovely like a Giacometti statue," he murmured.

"With those little metal bumps all over it?"

He snorted. "Perhaps without the bumps. I'll have to find out."

"Sounds fine to me." Her hips, thighs, knees, and

ankles were positively wobbly.

"To me, too. But first…soup."

"What? Soup?" As if she'd never heard the word before. *After what just happened, this is the right moment to be thinking about food? Is he crazy?*

Then, leaning in, he took her lips in a long, deep, soul-searing kiss, scattering her doubts, quashing any questions. "Soup, and sitting by the fire, and being here together, just the two of us. Let's take things very slowly." His voice was a low, bear-like growl that thrilled every teensy, tiny nerve in her body. "We have the whole night in front of us."

"How wonderful," she sighed.

Chapter Eighteen

The chirping of early birds woke her, and she snuggled more deeply into Michel's embrace, savoring the texture of his skin, the male scent of him. He was asleep, breathing evenly, his bristly chin against her forehead. He felt so strong, so safe…a curious sensation since she knew how temporary the situation was.

But what an exquisite experience this night had been; what a gentle, considerate lover he was, and how fervent her own response. She had suspected he would make her feel with more intensity than any other man, but this had brought loving to another dimension. And now it was over.

Time to get back to the château and start packing her things. She wondered if the others knew she had spent the night here. Azeline did, of course, for Michel had called to tell her that Callie was safe with him, and he would bring back her car tomorrow. So now what? Today was the last day of the retreat. Tomorrow, she would be heading for Paris, wasn't that her plan? It was.

She thought of the cafés she had wanted to sit in, the museums she'd longed to visit, and the taste of busy city life she had been looking forward to. Instead of anticipation, her heart felt as heavy as an old lead cannonball. She would be leaving all of this.

Michel stirred. She turned, saw he was awake,

watching her, and smiling. Then he leaned in, kissed her. "*Bonjour.*"

She couldn't believe the tenderness in his eyes. He had technique, seduction, and sexy mornings after down to a fine art. "*Bonjour* to you, too."

"What were you thinking about?"

Her heart quailed. "About how I have to scrape all my things together, pack them up, then start saying goodbye to everyone. I'm…supposed to be leaving for Paris…tomorrow." Even she heard the slight catch in her voice.

Pulling back, he propped himself up on one elbow. "Paris. That's what you're planning to do?"

"That's what I'd *originally* planned," she confirmed, although it didn't sound so enticing now. How much nicer it would be to stay here, in this low, stone house with its fabulous studio. With this heavenly, bear-like man. Of course, she couldn't say that. Wouldn't Michel think she was just a clingy female?

His expression had changed from pleasant to glowering. "I don't like one-night romances."

"Meaning what?" Her heart began pounding, but she tried to quash hope yet sound lighthearted. "One-night stands, we call them in English.

"It's the same thing," he growled.

"You're right." She slid her hand over his broad chest. "I don't like them either."

"Go back to Froideval, pack. Then come back here."

Her heart flip-flopped. "You mean that?"

"Of course, I mean that." He was still growling.

She sighed with pure happiness. "Your wish is my

command, big bear."

"Big bear?"

She almost laughed out loud but stopped when she saw his expression. Did he actually look uncertain?

"And your wish?" he asked quietly.

"It's very definitely my wish, too. But you said you're a lone wolf. Why would you want me hanging around?"

He grunted with exasperation. "Being a lone wolf doesn't mean I'm antisocial. It's just a way of protecting my privacy. It's very rewarding, being a known artist, but the last thing I enjoy is having people drop in to talk shop all the time. Art, art, art—if you hang around with the hangers-on, you start believing you're a star because no one treats you like a normal person. After that, you expect every single person you meet to behave in that same way toward you, and you lose touch with reality. That's lethal for any artist who is trying to do significant work."

"I know what you mean," she said, thinking of Nicholas, his groupies, and his flatterers.

"So that's settled." He was looking very chuffed. "I'll come by Froideval and pick you up at around four this afternoon." And he kissed her again, very soundly. And she kissed him back, her heart full. And then things became very intense indeed.

****

There was a farewell luncheon for the artists who were leaving that afternoon. Callie went up to her room to pack her things. When she was done, she inspected herself in the mirror for the last time. Remembering what Michel had said, she left her hair loose: *Relax, stop being so prim. Be casual, for once*. Wasn't her neat and prissy way of dressing just another hangover from her childhood? A rebellion against her mother's preference for floating, semi-transparent hippie dresses?

Time to let go of all those childhood neuroses. Pulling her pretty blouse out of the waistband of her skirt, she let it hang softly around her hips. Then, smirking, she undid the top two buttons and cinched in her waist with a belt. Okay, this was only a small step toward sexy-casual, but she'd get there eventually.

As she made her way down the stairway, she acknowledged how much she'd appreciated staying here, waking each morning to beauty. But as delightful as her time in Froideval had been, it could never compare to the unforgettable evening—and heavenly night—in Michel's arms. And soon, she'd be with him again!

She wanted to pirouette along the marble floor and swing from the chandeliers, but the sour, bewigged folks in the long rows of portraits were glaring at her most disapprovingly. *I don't blame you for being jealous; you're stuck here forever, glued into place by those thick coats of varnish and imprisoned by all the decorous gold frames.*

Some of her heady joy was dissipated by the sight of Azeline coming in her direction—after all, as Michel's sister, she might be terribly protective of him. But that woman's smile was as easy and friendly as usual. "How did you enjoy my brother's rustic peasant hut?"

Highly uncomfortable, Callie flushed. "It's hardly that," she riposted, ready to defend every square inch of that gray stone building. Then she realized Azeline was only teasing.

"I know," Azeline admitted. "It's an exceptional place that he has, snuggled into the hillside and surrounded by trees and wildflowers. I sometimes wish I could leave all this luxury in Froideval, go live humbly in a manageable house like that one. But that's only sometimes. The rest of the time I realize how lucky I am to have all this craftsmanship and history around me."

"You are lucky," Callie agreed. Then she shifted, uneasy; she had to let Azeline know she was about to fly the coop, and she couldn't think of a subtle way of doing so. "I've packed up my things. Tonight, I'm going back to Michel's house."

"Good for you," crowed Azeline with evident delight. "That should keep the ghastly Garance at bay."

Flabbergasted, Callie gaped at her. Then waited, hoping she would say more, give a hint, a tidbit, anything. But, laughing gaily, Azeline was already moving down the hall.

In the former servants' kitchen where everyone was gathered, she also saw Nicholas, but not his agent, that Monique Mottet. As Callie expected, he ignored her, for he now knew she was of no use to him, and she was relieved that he didn't single her out. He was someone she wouldn't miss, although there were a few others in the room she regretted saying goodbye to, particularly Laurent of the bloody paintings.

"You're leaving for Paris?" he asked.

"Some time in the next day or two, maybe," she answered, although her heart wasn't in it, not anymore. Paris, with its busy streets, noise, and crowded museums, couldn't hold a candle to these lanes and fields. What else would she miss? Her easy new friendship with Louis and Azeline—that was the downside of being in close contact with interesting people for a short time only. As for Michel...he would always be irreplaceable, and the sheer joy she'd felt when in his company would be reduced to memory. Fate had given her a break, but it was a transitory one.

Still, she was here now, she would be seeing Michel shortly, she would be in his arms tonight. At this very instant, life was ideal.

Telephone numbers were exchanged; there were promises to meet up, although she knew how unlikely such meetings were with people who lived in different corners of the country. Then, the meal over, she went to her room, fetched her bags, carried them downstairs, and waited for Michel on the stone steps.

The sun had successfully fought its way through the last shreds of low-hanging cloud, and the early blooms of black locust trees perfumed the air. Callie leaned back against the parapet and relished the wait...and it was a relatively long one. She soon understood why.

Instead of the chugging so-called antique van, it was the rattling wooden wagon pulled by Foumi that came into view. She couldn't help giggling. Trust Michel to arrive in style. Naturally, Romeo was there, too, and he gave his usual, highly exaggerated welcome, as if they hadn't seen each other just this morning.

With an entrance like this one, several artists tumbled out of the front door of Froideval, and they goggled with astonishment as well as envy as Michel slung her bags into the cart. Then, with a final wave, she, Michel, Romeo, Foumi, and the clanking cart headed out toward the line of trees.

"That certainly astounded everyone," she said when they were out of eyesight.

"It did," said Michel. He seemed to be very pleased with himself.

"I wonder what shocked them more—your arrival with a horse and cart, or my departure with you. If you ask me, I think I just made everyone terribly jealous."

Grinning wholeheartedly, he stopped, pulled her into his arms, and kissed her. Hearing her sigh of pleasure, he claimed her lips again, but with far more passion. She wound herself around him, her fingers weaving into the tight curls of hair at the back of his neck, one leg lifting, then curving around him. Arching back, she met him eye to eye, delighting in his gaze, in the happiness reflecting her own. *Black magic. That's what this is.*

At the house, she waited while he unhitched Foumi and gathered the several tools that were lying in the cart.

"You were out in the field working?"

"I was."

"You said planting season is over."

"I was taming a bramble hedge."

"Doing what?"

He smiled at her surprise. "Taming brambles means staying on friendly terms with prickly things."

"What for? Most people hate brambles."

"They do," he acknowledged. "They rip them out, burn and poison them, do all they can to get rid of them, but it's a losing battle. Brambles are resistant and adaptable, and they'll be around long after we humans have disappeared off the face of the earth. We should be working with them, leaving them as wild hedges, because they protect hedgehogs and nesting birds, their flowers provide bees and butterflies with pollen, and spiders and insects can live safely between their branches. All I do is make sure the brambles expand correctly and don't smother everything else."

Callie peeped at him from under her lashes. "Would you show me how to tame them, too?"

One eyebrow quirked. "Because?"

"Look," she said a little breathlessly. "There's a big part of my education that's missing. I don't know anything about planting, or growing things, or taming brambles, or anything at all, but I'd sincerely enjoy catching up, learning how to do those things."

"Okay, then." Although he didn't sound entirely convinced. "I don't mind having a working partner."

Her heart squeezed. A working partner? For a day? Two days? Three? *That's the problem with a budding relationship. You never know where you stand, or how and when things will end.*

Michel carried her bags into the house and returned with a table and two chairs. Soon they were sitting amongst the long untamed grasses growing around the house, drinking zesty white wine, and munching on olives that he had harvested and prepared.

Once again, Callie marveled at how easy conversation was with Michel. He was an amazingly attentive listener, and his love of storytelling encouraged her to shun banality and be as creative as he.

When evening's light chill finally set in, they went inside and sat by the fire, sluttishly slurping soup and forking salad from bowls on their knees. And that night, loving him, taking pleasure in his touch, rediscovering his scent and the taste of his skin, she seized on every second, stored it away in memory for when this interlude would be over, and she would be gone.

****

Sun was here in the morning, dancing merrily across the wooden farm table in the kitchen. Michel sat across from her, his expression unreadable. Callie's heart clenched, and carefully, she put down her coffee mug. Was this it? The end of the two-night stand? Why guess? Just grab the bull—or the bear, in this case—by its metaphorical horns.

"Michel? Is there something wrong? Are you feeling claustrophobic? Do you want to be alone?"

He glared at her. "You want to leave?"

"Only if you want me to. I mean…I could go to Paris."

"So you want to leave here and go to Paris, just as you planned?" he growled. "That's what you're saying?"

Callie tried hard, but she couldn't manage to fight back a grin. "I think this is what's called an international misunderstanding. No, I'd much rather stay here with you. Paris can wait."

He relaxed, and reaching for her hand, he turned it, kissed the palm, and curled her fingers through his. "People were living in Paris ten thousand years ago, so hopefully the city will be around for a while yet. However, I do have a problem."

"Go on. Tell me."

Releasing her hand, he leaned back in his chair and rubbed his face. Then met her eyes. "There's a painting I should be working on—a commission. But if I disappear into my studio the way I always do in the morning, I'll be neglecting you, my guest."

Callie let out her breath and relaxed. "That's your problem?"

He nodded.

"The only problem?"

Again, he nodded.

"And that's how you see me? As your guest?"

"That's what you are." A nerve ticked along his jaw, a sure sign of tension.

Standing, she moved over to his side of the table, sat down next to him and trailed one hand over his rough, unshaven cheek. How she loved touching him, being near him. Her heart turned over.

"How about this? We'll say I'm a lover, not a guest. I agree that guests always have to be entertained and taken places. We have to make sure they don't get disgruntled, or feel unwelcome, or neglected. But a lover is different."

"Go on." He was watching her closely.

"Lovers understand each other. They work in symbiosis, because they're partners." She leaned into him, trailed kisses along the hard-soft line of his jaw. Then pulled back and smiled at him. "Please, do us both a favor. Go to your atelier, paint, create, and be happy. I also have work to do—drawings I've been trying to perfect all week."

"You don't mind?"

"Haven't you been listening?" Callie tapped his big, broad shoulder. "I promise that I'll become grouchy and intractable if you treat me as a guest, force me to just hang around doing nothing else but sightseeing, gossiping, eating, and drinking bottles of lovely wine." *And falling in love*, she added, but didn't say.

****

How easy to adapt to Michel's daily routine without any sacrifice to herself. When he painted, he did so passionately, self-absorbed, and lost to the world. Sometimes, usually in the company of Romeo, she settled into the far corner of the atelier where, outside the open window, flowers and pale grasses waved, and spiders created silvery webs. Other times, she nestled under a mighty oak, studying the play of leaves, spying on birds, and listening to Foumi chaw weeds.

She worked as intently as Michel did, weaving her own patterns in pastel, creating tangles of shade and flashes of light, the faint scratchings of insects. She had never known she could do works like these, and whether they would please anyone in the big wide world no longer mattered to her. It was Michel's praise that touched her deeply. When he told her they were beautiful, she knew he meant it.

There were the afternoons out in the field, too, and under the sun's late spring light, they observed and trimmed. And today, knowing she understood how things were done, he'd left her on her own. She basked in the solitude, the cacophony of birds, and the knowledge that she was working with nature, not against it.

Closing her eyes, she lifted her face to the sun. How magical it was just sitting on the cushiony earth, clippers in one heavily gloved hand, and a barbed green bramble twig in the other. How lucky she was to be here. *I want to live this way for the rest of my life.* Now, at least, she knew what she wanted.

She wanted to continue digging in crumbly, brown earth, planting fragile saplings and encouraging them to grow sturdy and tall. She wanted to see branches become home to birds and insects, for roots to be safe havens for furry and scaled creatures. She knew there were people with these same aspirations in England, and when she returned home, she would seek them out, learn more, and participate. The thought gave her some comfort and soothed the ache in her heart.

She heard panting, and Romeo appeared from nowhere, wagging his tail, overjoyed at seeing her, although they'd been together just ten minutes before. She put down the clippers, pulled off the thick gardening gloves, and rubbed Romeo's fuzzy-rough head. Then watched Michel coming through the leafy passage between briars and nettles. How she adored that bear-like amble of his and his kindly steadiness. How she cherished the sheer pleasure he took in life.

His eyes were peaceful, even loving, as he settled down beside her. "Why are you grinning like that?"

She laughed out loud. "Because the first time I saw you in the train station, you reminded me of a big brown bear. And you still do."

He squinted at her, nonplussed. "A bear? Is that good or bad?"

"Believe me, it's wonderfully good. I also want to tell you how much I love being here, doing this sort of work. How lucky you are, Michel, to have all this around you all the time." She took in the hills, the oaks, and the regimental line of tall pointy poplars farther down the dale.

He watched her silently for a minute, his expression unreadable. "When were you planning to leave?" he asked.

Desolation clutched her stomach like an icy claw. Each day she had pushed this same wretched question out of her mind. Now it was right here, staring her smack in the face. She didn't want to think of departures. She wanted to stay here for forever, live in the savory green of nature, in the intensity of Michel. But life wasn't like that.

"I have to be back at work on Monday," she said with a distressing wobble, and she coughed to hide it.

He reached out, cupped her head in both hands. "Do you want to go back?"

She met his gaze squarely. "Of course I don't." *But dreams rarely become reality.*

He looked extremely satisfied. "Good."

"I love being here. I love working beside you." She caught her breath. "And I do love you."

"Then it's settled."

"What is?"

"I love you, you love me." His tone was very definite. "You want to stay here with me, I want you to stay. You see? It's really very simple."

His declaration was so stunning, she pulled away from him and pressed a hand to her heart. "Simple? How can you say that? How can I possibly stay? What will I do for work? For money?"

"I'm not very expensive to keep." Those marvelous creases around his eyes appeared. He was laughing at her, as he often did. "Callie? I do earn enough money to wine and dine you, but if you don't like the idea of being a kept woman, you can always teach art classes at Froideval. Or you can give conferences on pottery, or pastel. And you can start showing your work in galleries, see how that works out."

Move from London? Change countries? Give up her job at the museum? Change her life so radically? He said that would be simple? What a joke! She could only shake her head in disbelief. Then the other possibilities flowed in. Show her work? Wake up in Michel's arms every morning?

She met his steady gaze, the solid look of this good man she loved. He was right, she knew it. It could all be so simple—almost too simple to be part of real life.

"You know what they say, don't you?" she said, her throat tight with emotion. "When something sounds too good to be true, it usually is."

He laughed, a rousing belly laugh.

"What's so funny?"

"Wait until you see what daily life is like with a big brown bear."

A word about the author...

Writer, social critical artist, and impenitent teller of tall tales, J. Arlene Culiner was born in New York and raised in Toronto. She has crossed much of Europe on foot, has lived in a mud house on the Great Hungarian Plain, in a Bavarian castle, a Turkish cave dwelling, a haunted house on the English moors, and beside a Dutch canal. She now resides in a 400-year-old former inn in a French village of no interest where, much to local dismay, she protects spiders, snakes, and weeds. Observing people everywhere she goes, she eavesdrops on all private conversations and delights in hearing any nasty, funny, ridiculous, sad, romantic, or boastful story. And when she can't uncover any salacious gossip, she makes it up.

Author Websites https://www.j-arleneculiner.com
https://www.jill-culiner.com

Thank you for purchasing
this publication of The Wild Rose Press, Inc.

For questions or more information
contact us at
info@thewildrosepress.com.

The Wild Rose Press, Inc.
www.thewildrosepress.com